Advance Praise for *The Houseboat*

"*The Houseboat* is a worthy addition to the canon of country noir. Bahr's novel is eerie, dark, and disturbing in the best possible way." —Ivy Pochoda, author of *These Women*

"*The Houseboat* is a new noir classic. I loved it." —Tod Goldberg, author of *The Low Desert*

"*The Houseboat* is as taut and chilling as it is vivid and self-assured. Bahr delivers a gritty, page-turning debut not to be missed." —Jonathan Evison, author of *Legends of the North Cascades*

"Dane Bahr has written a classic mystery that propels his readers through the avenues, back roads, and waterways of a small town on a dire mission to sort through gossip and find the truth. A subtle and smartly paced psychological page-turner with characters you love for their flaws." —Sarah Gerard, author of *Binary Star*

"With scenes as propulsive as any found in *True Detective* and dialogue that could hold its own against the novels of Cormac McCarthy or Donald Ray Pollock, Dane Bahr's debut, *The Houseboat*, is truly a thing of beauty! Enticing the reader from the get-go, with a clear, clever, and ultimately haunting writing style, Bahr delivers on every page." —Urban Waite, author of *Sometimes the Wolf*

"With echoes as far-reaching as Raymond Chandler and James Salter, Bahr's work stands uniquely on its own." —Jarret Middleton, author of *Darkansas*

"*The Houseboat* will unsettle you, scare you, and break your heart. It's grimly authentic, bleak and beautiful. Its people wear the faces we see in our mirrors, and the ones we glimpse in our most terrifying dreams. It's a distinctly American gothic mystery—perfect reading for the Lovecraftian times we are living in."

—Molly Gloss, author of *The Jump-Off Creek* and *The Hearts of Horses*

"It'd be easy to mistake Rigby Sellers—the drifter at the center of Dane Bahr's *The Houseboat*—as an invention of Cormac McCarthy or William Gay, but it'd also be a mistake. Bahr has created a literary miscreant all his own, and for all the fright Rigby conjures—and there's plenty of it—he's as much a foil for the supposedly civilized small Iowa town he haunts as he is a spectacle unto himself. This book is as eerie and dark as a Mississippi river slough, and just as rank. You don't want to miss it."

—Peter Geye, author of *Northernmost*

"Dane Bahr has an unteachable knack to make the natural world a character. And once the book's ecosystems spring to vibrant life, there is a hell of a page-turner floating on top."

—Joshua Mohr, author of *Model Citizen*

"*The Houseboat* is an unruly, scarred and dusk-haunted book. In Bahr's stunning, transcendent descent into the old guilt of our collective humanity, something utterly unique awakens."

—Shann Ray, author of *Atomic Theory 7*

"*The Houseboat* is a little bit Eudora Welty, a splash of Edgar Allan Poe, and a whole lot of originality. Dane Bahr levels a landscapist's eye on 1960 Iowa and a gothic one on the human currents circulating in its cornfields, woods, and waterways. It's a wonderful juxtaposition of the bucolic and the horrifying."

—Glen Chamberlain, author of *Conjugations of the Verb To Be*

WITHDRAWN

THE HOUSEBOAT

A NOVEL

DANE BAHR

COUNTERPOINT
Berkeley, California

The Houseboat

Copyright © 2022 by Dane Bahr
First hardcover edition: 2022

Library of Congress Cataloging-in-Publication Data
Names: Bahr, Dane, author.
Title: The houseboat : a novel / Dane Bahr.
Description: First hardcover edition. | Berkeley, California : Counterpoint, 2022.
Identifiers: LCCN 2021018441 | ISBN 9781640095083 (hardcover) | ISBN 9781640095090 (ebook)
Subjects: GSAFD: Mystery fiction.
Classification: LCC PS3602.A465 H68 2022 | DDC 813/.6—dc23
LC record available at https://lccn.loc.gov/2021018441

Jacket design by Lexi Earle
Book design by Jordan Koluch

COUNTERPOINT
2560 Ninth Street, Suite 318
Berkeley, CA 94710
www.counterpointpress.com

Printed in the United States of America

10 9 8 7 6 5 4 3 2 1

For JB

. . . this desolation out here called forth all that was evil in human nature.

—O. E. RØLVAAG

THE HOUSEBOAT

Prologue

During the late summer of dry years in that valley of Iowa, when the rains were unreliable, the elm trees and bur oaks hardened and grayed with the dust of passing trucks on the county roads. All the green of the Allamakee Valley was dulled by that dust and a wilted look to everything appeared and the horses and the cows, dusted in their pastures, moved like ash blowing in a small wind. The little grass near the roads was short and brittle and the weeds rooted in the dry ground turned a dark green and pushed out along the dry earth. The leaves on the trees grew crisp and rattled on their branches. Ants scuttled in thin processions, dark rivulets on the tallow land, and grasshoppers clicked on their inadequate wings and ratcheted their long legs together in the narrow fields of bluestem. Tall clouds grew in the distance each afternoon, hopeful, but dropped their rains over another country, and the tractors crossing their fields drove the dust into the air. The evenings were golden and the settling dust gilded the sky. And the mornings were heralded with dew but the white sun quickly burned that away, and the river would slip through the lowest stones of the bed like a whisper. The bullfrogs huddled in their drying places and cried out wildly into the hot nights. The hardened prints of animals in the dry mud showed where the river had been, and the blanched logs of floods past told where it was going.

There was a saying among these people: A dry year will scare you to death, and a wet year will kill you.

In the wet years when the pale blue of the sky darkened and the big clouds, heavy with rain, came from the south and did not skirt the valley, the country changed. The air grew muggy. The dry county roads became cratered, slowly at first as the new rains came gently, and the coming rain gave a sweet smell. Mothers would come from their houses and call in their children and the men working their fields would pause, hooking their thumbs in their denim overalls or stoving their hands into the hip pockets, and face the darkening sky and sniff at the air.

The first rains cleaned the thin film of dust from the trucks and soon there was no dust at all. The county roads became gullied and sloppy with red mud and the trucks forded the slop. The men huddled with their arms crossed in the open bays of their barns and muttered crossly once in a while as the rain pounded down. During particularly wet years a group might gather at someone's place and in the barn they would set up picnic tables and hold a kind of impromptu social as a talisman to the rain. The women would bring pies and the children would chase each other through the barn, someone might bring a fiddle or a guitar, and a few might even dance, but you could see in the hard faces of the men the worry they carried like religion, and their eyes could not lie. The women would steal careful glances toward their men, sharing their worries, as they served the pies to the children, talismans themselves.

Two days of hard rain and the townspeople would watch the river turn brown as the water climbed its banks. Three days and the mayor would close the smaller bridges on the outskirts of town and the townspeople would begin to sandbag the south end. Four days of hard rain and the river became a butcher. It would rip at the banks as it swelled and cleave the edges of cropland like a knife to brisket. The rain fell and the river would feed. There was nothing it wouldn't take: trapping pigs and cows and gnawing on timber girders until the bridges collapsed on themselves. Days of that and no ease. Dawn would come but only because the world still turned. But the east would not pale like their prayers had asked for. A dawn rising like dusk, and no sun and no relent, and the children would not run to play in it like they first did, and as the day became dusk the sky would darken and night would fall quickly and still the rain came and the river butchering.

PART I

MINNEAPOLIS
1960

WITNESS #1

That was a strange time. Seems every fifty years or so yeh hear bout them kind a things happenin. Yeh can try to rationalize it, divvy er out. Put the blame wherever it makes yeh feel better bout it all. But it ain't the truth. All these things happenin now. I remember hearin bout Sheriff Fielding's cousin, Eli, down in Willow, that's jest north a Davenport, all em years ago when he was the newly lected sheriff, all em missin people and how it all turned out. That story makes yer skin crawl. Yeh know I'm goin to change what I said earlier bout it bein ever fifty years. Maybe it used to be ever fifty years but it's happenin more now it seems. The world's changin.

Here's a little somethin I told my sisternlaw. Twenty years ago, maybe twenty-five, she chewed me out bout my drinkin, said, Don't yeh want to live to see a hundern? Ain't yeh wantin to see them grandkids git married? Ain't yeh wantin to be a great grandaddy? I told er, if the lord cares fer me to see that age he'll let me. I told er a hundern ain't up to me. That's the way I feel anyway. The damn direction this world is goin, I'd consider myself lucky not to have to live through it.

1

The nine o'clock sun burned above the eastern horizon, churning a smoke on the surface of the Mississippi River. From his office window, Edward Ness, a handsome and almost tall man around thirty-five years old, watched the laminar bands of sunlight fall frayed through the avenues of downtown Minneapolis. The city sounds swelling up the buildings. Car horns. Vendors. A jet muffled overhead. Ness took his coffee at his desk and blew the steam from it. He had his polished shoes propped in an opened bottom drawer. This morning he wore a gray suit with the jacket hung on the back of the chair. His black tie was clipped to his shirt. He was clean-shaven and his blond hair was neatly in place.

He leaned back in his chair and rubbed his temples with one hand, attempting to work out the hangover. Then, giving up, he lifted a bottle of rye from under his feet, along with a bottle of aspirin, and unscrewed the top and poured a finger's worth into his coffee. The coffee was too hot to swallow down the pills so he just chewed the aspirin. He sat a moment with his eyes closed. Tapped the headline of the morning paper with his finger. Blew on the coffee. Then the phone rang.

This is Ness.

Mr Ness. This is Deputy Clinton down here in Oscar.

Oscar?

Yes sir.

Why have I heard that? Where the hell's Oscar?

Iowa, sir.

Iowa.

That's right.

This have something to do with that grave robbery?

No sir, Clinton said. I don't believe so. That was down in Cedar Rapids.

I see. Well. Ness leaned back and closed his eyes again. What can I do for you, Deputy?

Yeh get the mornin paper up there? The *Tribune* I think it is?

Looking at it right now, Ness said. He leaned forward in his chair and looked at the picture on the front page. The photo of a campground and the town's name in the caption. Ah, Oscar, he said. I see. Looks like you've got something going on down there.

I ain't got the foggiest what we got goin on down here, Clinton said. No one does.

You get in touch with the chief?

He's the one who recommended you.

Lucky me.

When can yeh get here?

How do you mean?

Chief said you were free.

He did, did he? Ness closed his eyes and rubbed them. How's the chief know about Oscar, Iowa?

He and the sheriff down here go way back, Clinton said. Fishing buddies and all that. Chief called us. A bit of a favor, I suppose.

You don't have anyone there? No one in . . . where's the next biggest town?

Des Moines.

Yeah, Des Moines. No one there?

No one as good anyway. Or so the sheriff and the chief say. Chief said it'd be good for yeh, whatever that means?

Did he? I see. Well, we all need salvation, don't we, Deputy?

Pardon?

Nothing. How long's the drive?

Three, four hours, if there ain't any traffic.

Ness leaned back in his chair again and looked out the window.

Don't you have any detectives kicking around down there in Oscar?

No sir, he said. Like I said, none any good anyway.

I see. Well, I guess I'll see you tomorrow morning. He was about to hang up when he suddenly spoke into the phone. Deputy? You there?

Sir?

Let me ask you one more thing.

All right.

You got any good, quiet hotels in that town of yours?

2

Seven years gone and every night the same dream: Ness is walking through a bright field with grass reaching his waist. It is windy and the grass is blowing. In the distance, wearing the same clothes he last saw them in, his wife and son are standing on a slight rise facing him. The hill is barren, only dirt, and as Ness comes closer he can see his wife's hands are bleeding. His son is holding his mother's hand so his hand is bloody too. Every night in the same dream he starts to run toward them. The grass, however, begins to have a current and holds him in place. He's close enough to see that his wife has a bullet hole over her heart. His son's shirt is stained in the same fashion. He hollers at them and at this point, every night in the same dream, a thunderclap and his wife and son disappear.

And every night he comes awake from dark to dark, his shirt

all full of sweat, his breath trying to catch up, and he goes to his kitchen where he keeps a calendar, and in the stale darkness marks an X over the day, and he doesn't know if he marks it for the dreams or to prove that he's still here.

Seven years since he lost them. What the policeman told him, via a witness, was that her purse had gotten snagged on her shoulder as the man tried to take it. He panicked and shot her. Out of horror of what he'd just committed, almost as an impulse, he shot the boy too. A petty crime turned worse. They found the purse on the sidewalk two blocks away. Her wallet was gone, the photos of her family in their thin plastic sheaths remained.

Ness was only twenty-eight at the time. His wife twenty-six. Their son, who was afraid of thunderstorms but liked the rain, was four. Ness thought about that often. Thought: Seven years ago Peter was still a baby, and seven years before that he wasn't even real.

Ness had never been a drinker before that point. Been drunk maybe once or twice. Got sick off cherry wine one summer night after graduation and that stopped it before it became a habit. In fact, he never lost control back then. Linn, his late wife, used to joke that he wouldn't do anything if a little fun was involved.

Seven years. What he couldn't fathom was that the world still turned. People still went to work and paid bills and cooked supper and made love. The earth still swung around the sun and he on it.

He had sold the old house in the north end of the city because some memories are like torture. He had arranged for movers but did not remember arranging it. Perhaps it was him, perhaps some secretary within the bureau. It seemed great swathes of time passed without a single recollection. He sat at his desk most mornings, still drunk, not saying a word until one morning someone said the wrong word, and he lost his temper and tumbled into a rage. He was put on leave, the captain and another agent having to nearly carry him down to the street where a cab waited to take him home.

Take some time, the captain said.

He said, Take a shower.

Get your head right, he said.

That was six years ago, the first anniversary of their deaths.

He was reckless in the months to follow. Crashed his car one afternoon into a field of cows, killing several Holsteins. Fist fights in bars he was now banned from. When he was reinstated he nearly beat a man to death during a suspected breaking and entering. The perpetrator, Ness later heard, was now confined to a wheelchair and had to eat his supper through a straw.

Not sober, but the drinking after that incident lessened to a degree. He found God for a time and then lost him again. Church, it seemed, was held too early. And one night with hands clasped, on his knees, he simply ran out of things to say. If there was a God, Ness thought, he'd heard this all before, and night after night the only thing Ness wanted couldn't be returned, so, rising from his knees, the only other thing he wanted was a drink and that was just down the street. And like religion, he swore he'd be better about it. And he was. He drank, but was reasonable. Not with the frequency or the amount, but in his demeanor, his temper. It was his secret that he would keep to himself.

For seven years the smallest darkness brought the terrible

image of Linn and Peter. He had seen them lying on the ground. They were each covered in a cloth. She under a size for adults, the boy a tiny one. That such a coroner's tarp could be so small seemed the greater tragedy.

The phone call had reached him by way of his secretary. Ness didn't see her standing in his door but he felt something, and when he turned in his chair and saw the look on her face his stomach balled up like a fist, and without her saying a word all the happiness and all the joy and all the pure memories he had collected were ripped away from him in an instant.

On the street was a crowd. Police cars with their lights going. He had to press through the horde. Some officers were restraining the crowd with their arms outstretched. When Ness tried to get through they said, Hey buddy, move along.

Ness said, No.

Said, Oh God no.

Hey buddy, what'd I just say?

Ness swung at him, knocking him to the ground. A few other officers falling in around him. It was the captain that pulled them off, cursing them as he did, tossing each officer away like a mongrel dog. It's the husband, the captain kept saying. The husband!

Torn collar, his lip with a thin slice of blood appearing, Ness stood over the tarps in disbelief. Kneeling beside his slain wife, he pulled back the corner. Her face, but pale. Like pallid sunlight through haze. His eyes welled. The tears finally spilling over the lids like water from a bucket. He pleaded. Then he went to pull back the corner of his son's tarp but the captain stopped him, said, Don't.

For seven years, in a blink's instant darkness, he can see it. The city, the shadows, the crowd, the tarps, the drawn and sallow face of his wife, but what he's tortured by most is his son under that small bit of canvas, lying completely still. For seven years he's been haunted by uncertainty.

3

Driving home that evening the mid-June sun was still high overhead. He was thinking about the town of Oscar, Iowa, a town he had never heard of. Thinking about the worry in Deputy Clinton's voice, thinking about what the hell was going on down there. But most of all Ness was thinking about a drink.

The air was humid, and if you could see far enough the horizon was smudged. To the west, great purple columns, like fat worms, took up all the air from earth to heaven, and within Ness could see daubed pops of lightning like shots from a pistol. Rain tonight, he said aloud.

On his way home he always made three stops. First to the liquor store for a fifth of whiskey, then to the florist for lilies. The final stop was a small cemetery with ancient oak trees overlooking the river. Here he'd find their plot and stand for a moment, saying nothing, only looking down, his shadow stubby or long depending on the season, and then he'd tell them about his day. Often it was mundane. Plain talk, what others listening in might think of as stupid. Other times his voice might spike with a little excitement. When he had said all he could, he'd lay down the lilies and, with a handkerchief, polish the little tin car they'd given Peter for his birthday. Then he'd kiss each headstone. The walk back to the car had not gotten any easier. He would walk slowly, reluctant to leave. Some days he would turn back to see if the lilies were still in place and see his shadow, sometimes stretching on, as if it too was reluctant to go.

Today was no different. He laid down the flowers and polished the toy car.

Crazy times, he said. So I'll be headed out of town for a while. Place called Oscar. Down in Iowa. I know how you don't like me talking about this stuff in front of Petey, so I won't. Just strange is all. I was reading about it in the paper. I'm not sure what to make of it.

Ness knelt down. Rubbed a thumb on the corner of the headstone. Looked around at the grass.

They're doing a good job keeping it clean around here, he said. Then he said, Kids are all out of school. Summer vacation. Petey would've been what? Eleven? What is that, fifth grade? Sixth? Anyway.

He stood.

Just wanted to come and let you know where I'll be. Won't be too long. I promise.

He put his hands in his pockets. He pursed his lips. Then in a very solemn but matter-of-fact way said,

Miss you two.

It was like he was talking to someone over the phone.

He kissed his fingertips and touched each headstone. Then he walked to his car without turning back to look.

Hours later, in his small, empty apartment, with the thunderstorm going and the fifth of whiskey half gone, he wondered why he didn't turn to look earlier that day. Then he thought about the lilies and how they were probably scattered and sodden over the lawn.

WITNESS #2

Till that day in the summer of 1960, no one outside the county had even heard of our town a Oscar. This town's about as plain as a white wall. Spectacular things are not why people move here, if they move here at all. People are born here, go to church here, get married here, and then die here. Like the winds off the prairie west of the valley, like the river, events pass through Oscar like gossip. We're churchgoers. Grateful. Virtuous. I don't know of a single one who asks for moren they need. So it's not melodramatic to say when them horrors started takin place a ripple of terror ran through here. No one really believes in ghosts, but that's what it felt like. Like there was ghosts a-hauntin.

4

Morning and the rain had stopped. Ness came reeling awake. He had slept fitfully. Tossing with the thunderclaps and fighting the current in the wheatfield of his dreams.

He peeled his eyes open. His temples were banging like a drum. The empty fifth had tipped from the bureau and was lying on the floor. In the trees outside his window a chorus of songbirds was chittering happily. A thing he'd sworn off time and again had returned. The headache, the malaise. A moment of great despair. He went to the bathroom, pissed, and washed his face. In the mirror stared a man with blood-rimmed eyes with pouches the color of plums.

Goddamnit, he said.

His holster was hanging on a hook near the door and he took

his pistol from it and went back to the bed and lay down on top of the sheets.

The birds were singing and the wind was coming through the window very gently and when it hit his skin felt cool as water. He was staring at the ceiling, at the same crack in the plaster he always did, and he thought about his wife and his son, and for another countless time he put the pistol to his temple and flexed his finger on the trigger. The hammer drew back and against the birds singing and the wind blowing it made only a faint, hollow pop as the hammer fell on an empty chamber. He dropped the gun.

Okay, he said.

Then he stood and washed his face again and got dressed and packed a suitcase.

5

The city receded like a shoreline at sea. The river was moving slowly under the bridge. The tires of his car tapped rhythmically over the expansion joints. He was driving southeast and the shadows were leaning against him with the sun still low in the morning sky.

The country grew lush and verdant. There were great tracts of ash and elm, and where there were no trees, acres of corn grew in perfect lines. The highway rose and fell among limestone. It was a beautiful place. He realized he hadn't driven through these parts in quite some time. The pastoral countryside made him wonder why he chose to live in the city at all. He began thinking about the reason he was even here, the murder of that boy, and it seemed hard to believe that a place such as this could hold such evils.

He passed through small towns with quaint names and tractor dealerships. Coming in the opposite direction outside of a little place called Preston was a horse and buggy plodding along down the highway's shoulder, and the bearded Amish at the reins held up a wizened hand in greeting. The woman beside him in her somber bonnet and plain dress wore an expression that could only be described as impervious. Ness watched them in the rearview mirror before they too receded in the dust and humidity, and when they flashed out of sight Ness couldn't help but think they had returned to a time that was very long ago.

He crossed the state line around noon. IOWA WELCOMES YOU. There were orange lilies in the ditches and lime-green ferns. A shot of goldfinches banked and rose as one in front of the car so close that it made Ness flinch. He passed an old farm with an old oak tree that stood twice as high as the house and from an outstretched limb hung a swing with a small boy pumping his legs and it made Ness think of Peter and the craving for a drink was so strong it hurt.

The valley into the town of Oscar was deep. It made Ness think of a canyon. A sign on the highway marked an overlook and Ness pulled off and parked the car and cut the engine and walked out a ways to where a wooden rail was built at the edge of a limestone cliff. He gripped the rail. The wood was old and splintery. He looked over the edge, down at the tops of trees, the serpentine river that seemed miles away. The height was dizzying. He leaned forward. The dazzling height made him think of falling. Like he always did from before he could remember, he pictured himself dropping through the air. No different than a stick or a rock nudged off the side. Simply dropping. A car passed out on the highway and broke his hallucination. With the car fled, he was left with only the sounds of the wind and birds and the droning of insects that gathered about him.

He had made a reservation at the Luther Hotel on Water Street. Three and a half hours in total. Parked the car along the curb in front of the hotel and sat there eyeing it, leaning forward over the wheel. It was a nice old hotel with carved stone and dark hardwood and he thought there might be a valet but there was not. He looked at himself in the rearview mirror, put on his hat and straightened his tie. He sat back and produced a flask from his jacket pocket and took a drink off it.

At the front desk Ness rang the little silver bell. Set his suitcase on the floor and looked around. Two elegant staircases wrapped gently up along each wall and the balustrades were of a hardwood he did not know. There were expensive carpets on the floor and long velvety sofas. Mahogany tables held vases of fresh lilies and he wondered if they could take those away. There was a bar and a restaurant off toward the back and the walls were wainscoted. A young woman came through a door behind the desk and looked to be finishing her lunch. She dabbed a napkin at the corners of her mouth and smiled with her lips closed. Her blonde hair was pulled into a ponytail and she wore a patterned blue dress and low-heeled shoes. Ness seemed to watch the way her hips moved as she came through the doorway.

Looks like I caught you at your lunch, Ness said.

Naw, said the girl. Just a snack. One a the ladies brought in some pie.

What kind of pie?

She covered her mouth with a small hand and picked her teeth with her tongue. She apologized. Blackberry, I think, she said, trying to swallow. Some type a berry. Shouldn't be eatin pie before I've had my dinner.

A little early for dinner, Ness said. He looked at his watch. Seems more like lunch to me.

Dinner is lunch, she said.

Is that so? Since when?

The girl smiled shyly.

I don't know, she said. Jest what we've always called it here, I guess. Dinner is lunch. Supper is dinner.

I'll have to remember that.

He smiled at her.

Say, she said, you're a bit chatty for a man with a wife.

She looked at his wedding ring.

No, he said. You smile like her is all. When she was younger. Got a nice smile.

She smiled again, demurred.

Well. Yeh here to check in?

Yes mam. Should be under Ness. Edward Ness.

She opened a large ledger and found his name. Pointed at it. Here you are, she said.

There I am.

From Minneapolis, she said, reading his information.

Yes mam.

She smiled and handed him the key.

What's your name anyway? Ness asked. I might be here for a while.

Heather, she said.

Like the flower.

Yes sir.

You know mine already, so you can leave out the sir, if you want.

Yes Mr Ness.

He was just about to leave when he turned and said,

That friend of yours brings in any coconut cream you be sure to call me down, okay?

His room was on the third floor looking south over Water Street. He climbed the stairs and unlocked the door and set his suitcase beside a small wooden desk and took off his hat, hanging it on a hook near the door. Tidied his hair with his fingers. He went to the bureau and turned over one of the glasses there on a tray and poured two fingers of whiskey from the flask, then crossed the room to the window and pushed the curtain aside. Opened the window with the heel of his hand. Warm wind carried the smell of the river and farms, the smell of cut grass and a little exhaust. He stood looking at the street below. A jewelry store. A meat market. On the corner, a drugstore with a soda fountain in the back. Beyond Water Street the greened copper dome of the courthouse stood on the hill. He took a long drink off the whiskey, then set it on the windowsill.

He removed his jacket and threw it on the bed. Eyed the spire of the courthouse a moment, then turned from the window and picked up the phone on the desk. Held the receiver in one hand, the box in the other, and pulled the cord from behind the desk and went back to the window. The curtain lifted in the wind.

The voice of the girl from the lobby came on, said, Front desk.

This is Edward Ness in room—that's right. Say, Heather, I was wondering if you could get me the number to the courthouse? Ness stood in silence for a second, staring out the window. He clutched the phone between his ear and shoulder and reached for his drink. The girl's voice came back. She read off the number and he said it back to her.

All right, he said. Thank you, darling.

He was about to hang up the phone when he said, Heather, you there?

Yes?

Say, how old are you?

Twenty-five.

I'm thirty-five.

Okay.

I saw a restaurant next to the lobby when I came in.

Yes.

Well, he said, if I may, maybe you'd like to have dinner—I mean supper, with me there tonight. What would someone like you say to that?

Supper? she said.

Sure.

Ain't yeh married, Mr Ness?

It's just a little food, Ness said. Not much fun to eat alone.

Well.

There was a pause.

Tell you what, Ness said. I'll be in the restaurant at six thirty.

If I see you, I see you. If not I'll stare out the window and wonder what the hell I'm doing wrong.

He heard her laugh through the phone.

That a yes? Ness asked.

That's a maybe.

Okay. I'll take a maybe.

Goodbye, Mr Ness.

WITNESS #3

*That's correct. I was the desk clerk at the hotel. He seemed real polite,
Mr Ness. What little I knew of him. A little flirty, but in a nice way.
But the town was real shook up, you know. It was comforting to have
someone from a big city like Minneapolis come down. And yeah, I knew
Hannah. Wasn't in my year, but I knew her good enough. Knew Billy
too. He was goin a go to U of I on a football scholarship. Isn't that sad?
That's why the town really welcomed that Mr Ness. He was goin a
find out what happened. But no, sorry I can't tell yeh more about him.
The rumors though sound like a horror story, don't they, how the whole
thing turned out.*

6

At six thirty he was waiting in the restaurant. There was a cocktail sweating on a paper napkin on the table in front of him. When the hostess asked if he had a preference on a table he pointed at the one farthest from the windows. A little dark back here, the hostess said as they went back. She said, I'll have them turn on some lights.

Don't worry, Ness said. That candle there is all the light I need.

Heather arrived at a quarter till with a clutch held in both hands in front of her. She was wearing a pretty blue dress that fell to her knees. She was wearing her hair down. He'd not seen them behind the desk, but now, standing in the open with nothing to hide behind, Ness noticed her good legs. The restaurant was mostly full and she stood there, looking for him, rising up on her toes as if searching for someone in a crowd. When she finally saw him she looked down in a bashful kind of way and smiled. Ness stood when she came over and pulled out the chair for her.

I was starting to wonder if I got stood up, Ness said.

I'm sorry for being late, she said.

She sat down and Ness took the chair at her elbow.

I couldn't find my earrings, she said.

Ness brushed back her hair. He said, Almost be a shame to put earrings in ears as nice as yours.

Her face flushed red. A few of the other patrons were looking in their direction.

There is going to be talk tomorrow, she said.

Why?

Because everybody knows everybody's business, and you're a married man on a business trip, and I'm in this dress . . .

It's a very nice dress.

It's a dress that'll make people talk.

Ness shrugged.

Like you said, it's business. We'll keep it professional.

The waitress came with a glass of wine. She set it down on the table.

Hi Heather, she said.

They exchanged embarrassed smiles, and then she went away.

I took the liberty of ordering for you. Though I believe it was a martini I ordered.

Rachel knows I can't stand gin.

Ah.

See? Heather said. Everyone knows everyone. What are you having?

Old fashioned, he said, but with brandy. Sweeter that way.

Ness raised his glass.

To business then.

She had nice breasts and the dress offered a bit of cleavage but Ness never looked down. Not once. It put her at ease. She let herself relax.

So, Heather said. What do you want to talk about?

How about you talk, Ness said, and I'll just listen.

Listen?

I like the sound of your voice.

Again her face went red.

What can you tell me about Hannah Dahl? Ness said.

Oh, Heather said, right to it.

Ness shrugged again. She said what she knew, which was very little. Her age, for example. The years that separated them kept things superficial. When he asked about William Rose it was much of the same.

I'm just trying to get a sense of them, Ness said. Any reasons why a young man like Rose would be murdered? Or why Hannah was found running down the road without her clothes on or—

Is this a date? Heather interrupted.

Date? Ness said. How do you mean?

He looked genuinely surprised.

I mean we're having supper, she said. I'm wearing this dress. You're wearing a tie.

I always wear a tie.

Then he caught her eyeing his wedding band.

How old are you again? he asked.

Twenty-five.

Twenty-five. That's a good year. He sat back and sipped his drink. You ever been married?

No.

Close?

I had a boyfriend. But then he went off to college and that was that.

Peter was only a year old then, Ness said. Back when I was twenty-five.

Who's Peter?

My son.

Yeh have a son too?

A look of immense guilt fell down her face.

Oh sure, Ness said. And Linnie was twenty-three.

Linnie. Is that her name?

Heather looked into her lap and was picking at her nail.

Linn, Ness said, but I call her Linnie. Linnie Ness. Got a nice ring to it, don't it? Kind of sing-songy.

Heather pushed away the wine and was about to stand and said, I shouldn't be here. I'm not that kind of girl.

Of course you should, Ness said. Why not?

Heather lowered her voice.

Because you're a married man with a son. I think they would mind me sitting here, talking to you the way I am.

What way's that?

Yeh know what way.

I doubt it.

You do? And why not?

They're dead, of course.

What?

Yes. Passed on. Both of them. You don't think I'd be the kind of guy to hit on a pretty young woman while spoken for? Do you? No, mam. Ness took another drink. They were murdered too. Just like that boy, Rose. I take it personally now when people are murdered without reason.

Heather covered her mouth and began to apologize, but Ness stopped her.

Linnie always said it depressed her to see people eating alone in restaurants, Ness said. You're doing her a big favor here. She had a dress that was almost exactly the same. Though I have to say I think she would be jealous of the cleavage.

That caught Heather off guard, but seeing the playful look on his face she began to laugh.

There we go, Ness said. Laughing, drinking, a proper date after all. I might even have to sneak a little kiss at the end of the night.

He winked at her.

He picked up a menu.

Point me in the direction of something good.

At the end of the evening, Ness told the waitress to bill it to his room. Heather tried to chip in, but Ness said, No, no. Outside the light was pink. There was a racetrack just outside of town and they could hear the stock cars rumbling.

Thought maybe I'd buy you some ice cream, Ness said.

Heavens, she said, I couldn't eat another bite.

Then maybe I walk you home? Ness said. There's a killer on the loose.

My car's jest right there, she said, pointing.

Then I'll walk you there.

He opened the door for her and before she got in she looked at him with her head cocked and said, Yer a bit of a looney, you know that?

Looney tuney, he said.

She looked down at the street. She said she appreciated the supper. Then she looked up at him in a certain way and said, Yeh still goin to try and sneak that kiss?

Ha, he said. I tell you what, darling, you keep that one in your back pocket.

Yeh promise?

I'd hate to get you in trouble. Everyone knows everything, you know.

She leaned in and kissed his cheek.

Let em talk, she said.

Then she got in her car and drove off. There wasn't any wind, and sometimes, over the distant rattle of stock cars, he could hear the birds. He watched until her car disappeared around a corner, then he clucked his tongue and went in search of a bar.

1

In the morning Ness left the key to his room on the front desk
and crossed Water Street and bought a paper and went into Deb's
Café for his breakfast. It had rained the night before but it was
very bright now and the streets were smoking. He took a seat near
the window and the sunlight winked on the car hoods. Set his hat
in the booth beside him and brushed his hair down. A waitress
came and stood with arms akimbo. A pleasant look on her face as
though she knew him.

Well, she said. How you?

She was maybe forty-five years old with dyed auburn hair
pulled up, a powder-blue uniform, and a white apron over the
front of her skirt. He ordered eggs and toast and when he finished
he went to the counter to pay. He pulled out his wallet and tapped

the bills laid on the glasstop and slid them over. He said, Is there a good barber in town?

Of course, sweetheart, she said. Ralph Lander.

I'd be obliged if you could point me in that direction.

Jest down Water there. On the corner.

Does he do manicures?

Heavens no, she said. He don't have no manicurist. She reached for his hand and turned it over and held his fingertips and examined his nails. I wouldn't worry about that, though. She winked, sliding his change over the counter.

Thank you . . . Millie, Ness said, leaning in to read her name tag. I like that name.

He left a dollar on the glass for her.

Yeh come back, she said.

You'll see me again.

That a promise?

It's the only thing I seem to make, Ness said, and he winked at her as he went out.

Ness went down Water Street. The air was thick and smelled like cows. He passed a newspaper rack and glanced at the front page and backpedaled and squatted down to read the headline.

Hmm, he said.

He fished several coins from his pocket and opened the glass door. Standing on the sidewalk, he read the entire article about William Rose and Hannah Dahl. When he finished it, he said Hmm again and folded up the story and tossed the rest of the paper in trash.

Further on, Ness opened the door at Lander's Barbershop. A small silver bell called over the door. Lander was sitting in the only chair reading the paper. He stood when Ness entered, folding the paper and setting it on the table under the mirror next to the combs and scissors and bottles of aftershave and pomade.

Yes sir, Lander said. Can I do for yeh?

Shave and a shine, Ness said. You don't do manicures?

No sir. Jest cuts and shaves. No shines neither.

Ness nodded. Hung his hat on a coat-tree. Laid his jacket aside and climbed into the chair. He turned his head to the left and right as though he couldn't make up his mind.

Lander was in his fifties. A small man with black and gray hair, a green tattoo on his forearm from his days in the service. Navy, Lander said, catching Ness eyeing it. He swept a faded yellow apron over Ness and tied it around his neck.

You serve? Lander asked.

Me? Oh sure.

Helluva theater, Lander said.

Some bad actors.

Ha! Lander said. I like that. Bad actors. You betcha. So what're we doin here?

Just a shave will be fine, Ness said.

Lander turned his head. Think yeh need a trim, son. Gettin shaggy round the ears. Trim to match the shave?

All right.

Hold on there a minute, Lander said. He came back with a steaming towel and wrapped it about Ness's face and tilted back the chair and spun him away from the mirror. Ness closed his eyes and listened to the razor on the strop.

Supposin yeh heard bout that girl they found? Lander asked.

Ness spoke through the towel. That's why I'm here.

You wouldn't happen to be that detective the sheriff called in?

Edward Ness.

Ralph Lander. Nice to meet yeh.

Lander removed the towel and lathered a brush in a warm eucalyptus-scented cream. Painted his face with it and then gently stripped it away with the razor.

Creepy stuff, Lander said. Some maniac on the loose.

Mmm.

When he was finished, Lander flung away the apron and spun the chair toward the mirror.

Damn fine sight yeh are, son, Lander said, brushing off his shoulders with a hand broom.

Thank you, Ness said. He looked down at his shoes. Wouldn't complain to a shine.

I'd give yeh one if I could, Lander said. Then he helped Ness on with his jacket. That'll be a dollar twenty.

8

Ness made his way up the hill toward the courthouse. Ten thirty. His jacket draped over his shoulder in the early heat. Nodded to a woman pushing a pram. Concrete streets becoming brick the closer he came to the government building. Tall maples, tall oaks. A sky the color of blue eyes.

At the steps of the courthouse he dabbed the sweat at his brow with a handkerchief. Then he climbed the granite stairs to a set of huge wooden doors. A meager wind made its way into the valley but brought nothing for the heat. Only ten thirty in the morning and already his shirt damp with sweat. He passed some government men on the stairs, said, Morning.

He walked down a long hall with placards of past mayors and councilmen. There was no air conditioning and the building was warm and awhirl with ceiling fans. His shoes sounded on the floor, echoing like a chamber. At the end of the hall a woman sat behind a wide dark-stained desk. She was on the phone, watching him as he approached. She smiled, said something into the phone and then hung up.

Good morning, she said.

Morning to yourself, Ness said. Looking for the sheriff's office. Seem to be a bit lost.

She pointed to her right, said, Looks like yer right where yeh need to be.

A pebbled glass door with a star printed on it. The name SHERIFF AMOS FIELDING stamped below.

No one's above the law, Ness thought.

You got an appointment? she asked.

I hope so. Drove three and one half hours to get here. Ed Ness. Your deputy gave me a call yesterday.

Oh! The detective from Minneapolis.

She gave him a look.

I know that look, Ness said.

She's a sweet girl, ain't she? That Heather.

She wasn't kidding.

Kidding about what?

About it spreading like a grease fire.

She looked at his wedding ring.

Ness held up his hand. Widower, he said.

At the first look of sympathy Ness held up his hand, said, No, no, none of that.

Well, she said, Heather is a very sweet girl.

Yes, Ness said. Noted.

Anyways, we're so happy to have yeh come down. This town ain't seen nothin like this before.

So I gather.

I'm Betsy, she said, extending a hand.

Ed Ness. But you already know that.

She gestured with her chin to a row of chairs just outside the sheriff's office. Have a seat, she said. He's with someone now. Some woman lost her cat up a tree.

Isn't that quaint, he said with a smile.

Yeh want some coffee? Tea?

I just had my coffee down at Deb's so I'm fine just the way I am. Thank you kindly though.

After some time a plump old woman in a shapeless green dress exited the sheriff's office. Her lips were brightly rouged and she wore a cravat that looked to be cut from the same bolt of cloth as the dress. She stood at the desk a moment, talking to Betsy. Mild distress. Ness heard her say: But if he's not goin to get him down, who will I call? Then she said something about church then thanked Betsy and then shuffled her way on thick ankles down the hall.

Betsy came around her desk and opened the door for him. She leaned in and said: Mr Ness for yeh, Sheriff.

Fielding, at his desk going over paperwork, looked up at the pair darkening his doorway. He set down his pen and thanked her. She closed the door behind Ness. Sheriff Fielding stood. Pulled up on his belt. Came from behind his desk and shook Ness's hand.

Detective Ness, Fielding said. What's the news?

I'm not sure to be honest with you.

Damn right on that. Yeh have a seat. Yeh want some coffee? I'll get yeh some coffee.

Thank you, no. Had my fill at the café just now.

Naw. Naw. No trouble.

He went to the door and called for two coffees. Then he closed the door and sat back at his desk. Sheriff Amos Fielding. A paunchy man in his mid-forties and judging by the shape he was in one could tell he'd gotten accustomed to being chauffeured around. Handsome enough. Played quarterback in another life. Wide shoulders, big hands.

He propped his feet in an open drawer. He never wore a tie and rubbed the skin at his throat. He shook his head. Spoke slowly in a low voice.

This whole goddamn thing, Detective. I don't know what to make of it. He pointed to a holstered revolver hanging on a hook in the wall. Started wearin that thing around with me. Cain't believe it. Carryin it around people that've known me since I was a boy. I been sheriff of this town since I was twenty-one years old. Can yeh believe that? Twenty-three years I ain't ever carried a gun on duty. Now this damn nonsense starts happenin. Pardon my French. He shook his head. I don't know, Mr Ness. We're dealin with somethin new here.

Why don't you call me Ed. I've a feeling we might be spending some time together.

That sounds good, the sheriff said. Amos Fielding.

Ness looked around the office. There was a placard made out in Fielding's honor for his years of service to the town. A picture of his wife. A stuffed bass over the window. The mount of a ten-point buck. There was a vinyl sofa along the far wall, a filing cabinet, a typewriter draped in a plastic dust cover, a small fan whirring in the warm air.

Fielding pointed.

Caught that monster there a few years back. Twelve-pounder. Yeh fish, Ed?

When I can.

We'll go. I know a good place. The sloughs round here got some nice fatties that'll take anythin yeh throw at em.

Uh-huh.

Then he pointed to the deer head.

That there's Bob. Don't know why I named him. Tagged that beauty the last time me and my deddy went out together. The fall before he died.

Was his name Bob? Your dad?

No it wasn't. Roger. But that's good. Shoulda named it Roger.

He turned the photo in the frame.

That's my wife there, he said. Sara. Been sweethearts since high school. You married, Ed?

No, sir, I am not. Widower.

Ness wondered if it would be more convenient to take off the ring while he was here.

Well I imagine the big city keeps you occupied.

Fielding raised his eyebrows but said nothing more and Ness appreciated the lack of questions over it.

Something like that, Ness said.

Sure. Well enough dilly-dallying, Fielding said. Here's what I know. The scuttlebutt is that Dahl girl, Hannah, she ain't left her room in three days. Ain't said moren a sentence to anybody. Fielding tossed a folder of photographs and statements across the desk. That's what we got so far.

Any word on a body? Ness asked.

The boy's yeh mean? Nothin.

Ness opened the folder and leafed through the contents. He read down the list.

Says here you have a suspect?

Where's that? Fielding sat forward and leaned his weight over the desk.

Ness turned the folder and tapped it out.

Suspect might be a little wishful a word, Fielding said. There's a feller who lives up that slough them kids were campin at. Only one who might've been in the area.

What's his name?

Rigby Sellers.

What's he like?

PART II

OSCAR 1959

WITNESS #4

Rigby Sellers was indeed a weirdn. I don't know much about him and I'd jest assume keep it that way. When Don was the manager at Wallace Tire n Brake down there in Guttenburg, he told me he had to fire Rigby cause he walked in on him one mornin doin some odd things against one a them tire balancer machines. Pants around his ankles. That still gets me evertime I think about it. Makes me shake my head. Some thins is just too weird not to laugh at. I heard Rigby put up a stink about gettin fired. Busted up some stuff, some little threats. Don had to write up a report claimin Rigby a kind of deviant. I think that's the word they used. But I ain't carin enough to know anymore.

9

The houseboat tugged gently at its ragged lines in the slough of the river. Braided rope moaning in the chocks. Floating nameless. It was a dilapidated thing constructed out of scrapwood and sheets of corrugated tin patched together. Stains of rust bleeding toward the sagging decks. Its ports rotten in their sashes. Threadbare sheets as drapes. The tarpaper roof, buckled and peeled, was left to wilt in the heat. A canvas tarpaulin here and there, nailed to the eave or weighted by castoff tires. The water swirling between the bank and the houseboat was brown with waste. Bits of trash would bob into sight, scum coated, half decayed, then fall below the surface again. Soiled condoms worming palely from the depths. Dead fish pirouetting in the stir, yellowed bellies bloated and skyward. A wooden skiff was tied to the transom.

The diminished noises of town just beyond the bend of the

river grew up softly from over the trees. Save for that the only sound was the water against the hull. A bird or two in the woods.

In this quietude the door of the houseboat swung open in a fury and out stepped a small man of around thirty years old carrying a bag of trash. He was dressed in stained canvas trousers, repaired with patches of various fabrics, held up with a set of black leather suspenders. Wore a red union suit underneath and it was unbuttoned at the neck. The smell like humidity.

He was thin and almost hairless. The slats of his ribcage threatening to burst the skin. The hair on his head grew like strands of eelgrass. He had dark pebbly eyes that didn't see well. Coke-bottle glasses that he probably found somewhere. A jutting brow and a bent nose, a patchy beard and an incomplete set of long jaundiced teeth. This unkempt man stumbled from the door and made his way around the deck toward the bank. Muttering something. In a clumsy motion flung the bag onto the bank where it exploded its contents, scaring up a vocal murder of crows beyond the brush. The trash slid toward the river, coming to rest alongside other such garbage snared in the dense bracken. The crows sat mocking him in the trees. Rigby Sellers.

He crossed the gangplank, stepping heavily onto dry land. Climbed the bank and made his way to a stand of oak where he dropped his patchwork trousers and squatted. Crows called in the trees. A rank smell grew into the muggy air and when he finished he wiped himself with a handful of leaves. He stood a moment contemplating some dull thought, his dark eyes gazing through those ridiculous glasses into the caged forest where strands of sunlight slanted like thread and he shifted his stare toward his stool where black flies already leaped in a viscid ballet. He took up a stick and poked at the shit. Flies scattered like black embers.

Back in the cool half-dark of his boat, he uncorked a jug and poured a generous amount of something fiery into a chipped mug. Tilted that back and then had another.

The houseboat was one-roomed. Cobbled together in a derelict's dream. Roof leaked and brown stains had run toward the floor, boiling the green wallpaper. Plywood floors he rarely swept. Aluminum folding chairs. A supper table hauled from the dump. There was a bare twin mattress set on the floor in the corner of the room and because of the houseboat's list he often dreamt he was on the high seas sinking. For a coffee table, he'd gathered a road sign and set it atop four cinder blocks. He bathed maybe weekly—riverwise in the summer, the bucket and sponge during colder times.

His one prize was a mannequin with long legs and wooden lips. He'd often talk to her. Sometimes try to feed her. He had bored holes in all the normal womanly places and sanded the edges smooth with a scrap of sandpaper. Painted in nipples and a triangle of pubic hair, the filigree of unkempt strands. He'd fixed her up so she came apart at the waist and he'd clean her out sometimes by flinging her into the river with a towline. He had a box of ladies' garments of all kinds and he'd dress her up and comb his fingers through her abrasive hair and tell her how pretty she was. At night he'd talk to her like she was capable of answering.

Now, at the kitchen sink, he watched through the warped windowpane a heron hunting. The bird on one foot, Rigby attempting to mimic, only to come crashing onto the floor, spilling his whiskey and cursing the bird. He staggered to his feet, wiping the burning wet from his chest and arms, and refilled his mug. Eyed the heron again and held his hand in the shape of a pistol and aimed it.

Dead bird, he said.

10

As a young man, in the boxcar of a train, Rigby Sellers wandered the lost areas of a country few have seen. Peering through the open door while the track ribboned on and the steel wheels thrummed over the rails. Seven years gone. During those years he ate when food was available and slept when he was tired. He was a thief but only because he had to be. Wandering seemed to suit him and he was good at it. The open country was freedom.

Those early years. Men like him. Friendships, if they can even be called that, were forged. Lasting anywhere from an hour to a couple of days. They brought their stories to the camps and passed around cautionary tales like whiskey. Towns to stay out of. Cathouses with diseased women. Sections of track unsafe to travel.

Rigby went south and the temperatures warmed. In St. Louis he was picked up for vagrancy and spent a week in jail. Here he was reacquainted with the hate and anger and jealousy of poor men. Here he felt the first sensation that the world was changing. Would never change. In April of '54 he was let out and immediately picked up again.

Another sentence. Another penance. Year on a chain gang.

Sent to a workhouse outside of St. Louis, he worked shackled to other men in all kinds of weather. Slept badly and ate worse. His body seemed to reject any nourishment it was given. At four in the morning to a different kind of reveille the prisoners were woken and loaded into hard-benched trucks and driven out to the country. Hot days. Bleeding hands. The daylong men with shotguns stood watch as Rigby worked in the ditches with his crude implement at God knows what. Men on horseback patrolling the road. Rifles resting upright on their thighs. Rigby learned a different way here, a sentiment of madmen.

Toward the end of his year Rigby had become something else. He began to take joy in seeing gentler men be punished. It was not perverse to see a weeping man, fresh off the town, the scents of cologne and whiskey and women still lingering, clubbed by a guard or prisoner until he begged. Quite the contrary. Rigby grew silent and slouched against the wall with a mad gleam in his eye as he watched the club come bashing down. Then after the beating had quit Rigby would blink dully and walk away.

When he was released for the final time he bought a new set of cheap clothes, a bus ticket, and went to Iowa. Got a job at a tire shop and was fired. With his remaining money he purchased a rotting houseboat where he reflected on the people and things that led to his abandonment, numbly watching the sun drift through the sky. Seasons changed.

WITNESS #5

That was the feller I seen. I remember him. He was pullin it in a wagon. I remember that cause I ain't never seen a man pullin a kiddy's wagon before. We came up on him in the car and I told Hugh to roll down his window. I asked the boy what he had in that wagon there. But yeh could see it plain as day. It was separated in two places, the legs of it stickin out like pieces of timber. Hugh asked him what he was doin with that there mannequin. He tell us somethin, I don't remember what now. I do remember seein a wood box filled with tools. There was some sandpaper and a brace. We asked him if he needed a ride, told him we could put that wagon and doll in the back, but he just waved us on. Mumbled somethin. He was a queer sort of boy. Only other time I heard his name said was that time that couple was kilt up near the quarry, when the sheriff issued that statement bout him. But that was a long time ago now. I don't know where he's at. I don't know.

11

He'd been to town all day combing through the Salvation Army's metal racks of women's clothing. In the store a doughy woman with platinum blonde hair asked him if he needed any help.

No I do not, Rigby had said sharply.

He had several items draped over his elbow and the woman looked there and felt at the blousy material. That's a nicen there, she said. Rigby recoiled.

Yeh keep yer fat fingers off her dress, he said.

Sir?

Yeh heard me! Keep yer cunt grease fingers off it. Don't want yeh ruinin it fore she has a chance a tryin it on.

She took a step back, going red. Went away.

His bony fingers worked madly at the hangers. He'd found two pieces. One a polka dot dress cut low in the front and the other a silky black chemise slip with a lacy hem. Mistook this for a dress for he knew no better. Held it out in front of him at arm's length and nodded secretively at how high it would rise on the mannequin's stiff legs.

He paced the aisles of recycled clothing and pictured what he would like to see her in. One little boy stood near a shelf of orphaned toys and when Rigby swung his eyes and found him staring he hunched and growled like a dog and it made him happy to see that he had scared the little boy.

At a circular rack in the back corner of the store he found the underwear. Little see-through pieces hung on thin straps. All kinds of colors. He dangled a pale blue corset from its hanger, the stocking suspenders pinned up. He hung that over his arm and pulled through the other items. Found a white suspender belt and took that too. A pair of black stockings caught his eye and he fetched them up and stretched them between his hands, testing at something, then balled the stockings in his palm and sniffed them. The chubby saleswoman passed, avoiding his attention, but he called to her. She came but stood a small distance from him.

Can I help yeh? she asked timidly.

Why yeh think I called yeh?

Okay. The woman had laced her thick fingers together and she stood looking down at them.

Yeh got anythin like Sophia Loren would wear? Rigby asked.

Sophia Loren?

He held up the corset. Sumpin like thisn here but smaller and black. Sumpin yeh can see through.

She looked at the black chemise slip in his arms. That looks pretty close to me. I think I've seen a movie where she wears something like that in it.

Goddamnit, said Rigby. I guess they plumb run out a people to hire when they took on you. Here. Take thesens to the counter and ring em up. Yer wastin my time.

12

Heading out of town he rested on a bench that overlooked the river. Closed his eyes and took in the sun like a snake. Drifted about in a light nap till the sound of voices stirred him and he peeled his lids open.

A group of boys sat huddled under the bridge below him, circled around like men squatting at a fire. Rigby watched them a moment. One of the boys held the magazine out and the folded page of a centerfold girl fell open. A hushed roar spread through the boys. They punched each other's arms. Rigby stood and made his way to a narrow footpath. The grass was waist high and grasshoppers sprung from everywhere. The boys were taken with their prize and did not see Rigby approaching. When Rigby spoke they all startled. The one holding the magazine snapped it behind his back. He was maybe fourteen years old with short blond hair.

Whatch yeh got there behind yeh? Rigby asked.

Each face was flushed in color and their eyes wide. They wore white T-shirts tucked into blue jeans rolled at the cuffs.

Nothin mister, said the one.

Bullshit, said Rigby. Hand me that magazine.

I can't. It ain't mine to give.

Then yeh shouldn't have it in the first place, yeh little shit. Give it here now. Ain't goin a ask it again.

The boy sat on the magazine. It's my brother's, he said. I can't let you have it.

Patience ran out of Rigby and he stepped into the circle of boys and reached behind the one and took his thin wrist in his hand. The other boys scooted away like rippled water.

Yeh give me that goddamn magazine boy.

Snatched the magazine from the boy's hand and glanced at the cover. A curvy redhead lay naked on her stomach across a bed with a foot kicked into the air. A charming little grin. Emerald eyes. The boy protested, and when he stood to retrieve the magazine, Rigby hit him in the mouth with an open hand, sending the boy to sit in the dirt. The others stayed seated.

This is filth, said Rigby. Ain't fer boys.

He folded the magazine and stuck it in his back pocket. Turned and walked out onto the path again. The hit boy called something after him but Rigby didn't hear it and he didn't turn around.

That night, with the sound of rain on the roof and thunder in the hills, Rigby searched the magazine for the picture he liked best. When he found it he laid the spine open on the table for studying and went to his doll. He chose a picture of the auburn cover girl lying in bed with a silk sheet draped about her hips, just covering the nipple of her breast. He laid the doll on the mattress and flung the blanket over her rigid hip then stood back and cut his eyes between the picture and the doll. He arranged the blanket in several ways. It never looked right. Frustration got the better of him and he took up the magazine and opened the stove door and pitched the magazine in. A thin tongue of green fire caught the page's edge and began to lick its way down. He could see the fire's light shifting on the glossy image of the woman's body through the open door. Changed his mind and reached into the fire and hauled the burning magazine from it. He let it drop to the floor where he stomped out the flame. Blackened pieces of ash wheeled like paper bats.

He chose another picture and tried the doll against that but finally went back to the original. Pulled down a sheet at the window to drape over her hip and turned down the wick in the oil lamp and resolved that it looked pretty good. He had a box of wigs near the bed and he fished through it till he found a red one and he put that on her. The centerfold's name was Mary Belle. Spoke that name quietly as he looked at the burned photograph. Got undressed and for the first time said her name.

13

Thirty years before, Rigby was born to a girl named Lila DeWitt. No more than fifteen years old. Night of his birth. November of 1931. Little north of St. Louis, Missouri. That ancient agony gripped her swollen abdomen and soon he was born. The other girls of the house stood gathered in the corners of the room, occupying the shadows. They crept into the doorway when they heard the wailing, to stand hushing each other, hands to their mouths. Lank ones, chubby ones, some prettier than you might expect. The madam more than once turned and said, See what carelessness gits yeh girls?

By the time the doctor arrived the child had already been swaddled loosely and the mother nearly bled to death, nearly carried off by the very thing she'd given life. At the sight of the wide oval of blood pooled on the sheets under the girl, the doctor hissed the madam away. Lila, colorless now, pale as her pillow, wallowed. Her eyes lolled like a drugged dog. The doctor massaged the uterine area. When that did nothing he got the girl into a Trendelenburg position and when that did no good he finally administered an IV. When the bleeding stopped the doctor wiped the sweat at his upper lip and turned to the madam.

How old's the girl?

She's nineteen, the madam answered.

The doctor shook his head in disgust. She ain't nineteen, he said. He looked to the far wall where a girl was holding the child. How he howled! Wrapped in a towel. He went to the girl and snapped his fingers. Give him here, he said. Brought the baby to the bedside. He spoke again to the madam.

What's this girl's name? Don't you tell me no more lies.

Lila, the madam said. Lila DeWitt. And that's the truth.

The doctor spoke soft now, fatherly. Lila, he said. Miss DeWitt, do you know who this child's deddy is?

When the girl didn't answer the madam said, Sellers. Lucas Sellers. But he ain't around.

The doctor said, Miss DeWitt, would you like to hold your baby? As he suggested the baby into her arms she held out her hands as though refusing a cup of tea. Turned toward the window to cry.

The madam and several girls stayed with the new mother well into the early hours of morning. Lila gazed absently at a candle burning on the bedside table. The baby slept near her side, cooing and making the sounds babies will.

Have you thought of a name? the madam asked. You'll have to call him somethin.

But Lila would not utter a sound.

When the first colors of morning paled the glass of the window, the bed was empty save for the swaddled child, kicking his small feet against the soiled towel. It was his cries, like the lost bleating of a small sheep, that woke the madam from her chair to find him there alone. The madam's father had been named Rigby. So that's what she called him.

The years passed. From infant to toddler, he took his first steps down the hall among the girls and dishonest men. The ones who had the night off would tickle his belly and chase him about their empty rooms to laugh and giggle. Sometimes they read him stories. Busy nights he spent alone upstairs playing with the rag dolls the girls had made for him. One regular brought the boy a wooden rifle. One night when he was six years old a door was left open by mistake and through the crack the boy saw the buttocks of a man he did not know thrusting against the backside of one of the girls. She said things to the man the boy didn't understand. It was frightening but he also could not look away. The next night he spied on a tall girl riding atop a man whose big feet hung off the end of the bed. Thought of the man like a horse. In the drawn candlelight another girl rose naked from a chair and began kissing the girl riding the man.

Fall of '37. The madam enrolled the boy in school but he never went. By the time he was twelve years old he could only read a handful of words. The names of the girls. Cuss words the regulars spelled out on damp paper napkins. Then late summer of '45. End of the war. Fireworks in the sky. Songs in the streets. One of the girls, porcelain skin and red hair, drank too much and found the boy watching the exploding colors through the paned window of the room once his mother's. Closing the door she slipped the robe from her shoulders. Seeing his excited state, she led him to her bed. It did not last long, of course, and in the morning she kissed him on the cheek and said she'd cut out his tongue if he told anyone. Fourteen years old. His first and last with a real live woman.

That same year the house was raided and he ran into the cold darkness of the woods, turning once to see the madam being taken away in handcuffs. The other girls, some in silk slips, some naked save for woolen overcoats. Then turning to run again, deeper into the woods, into darkness. He never did return.

14

He stood outside the glass storefront with his thumbs hooked in his overalls, gazing in at the tall mannequin in a black dress, speaking in a low mutter, if speaking at all. This one had a longer neck than the one he had now and that appealed to him. Green eyes painted on and he watched them as if she might suddenly look down.

At the door of the storefront a woman and child were coming out. Rigby opened the glass door, and expecting this man to hold it for them, the woman and child came through only for Rigby to trip over the boy.

Damnit boy! Rigby shouted.

Excuse me, said the woman. Don't you curse in front of my son that way.

Goddamn yeh too! Rigby said, stepping over the fallen child and entering the store.

The girl behind the counter was watching him as he came in. He crossed before the sales rack and stood inspecting the mannequin. He turned to the girl at the till.

How much fer thisn here? he asked. He'd said it loudly and some other patrons had looked up. The girl glanced at the other shoppers and came from behind the counter with her eyes cast down in embarrassment. Spoke in quiet tones as if to set an example. But he either didn't notice or he didn't care.

How much fer thisn? he said again.

She reached for the tag and spun it on its piece of string.

It's three dollars, she said. She was a shy thing, probably no more than fifteen years old. She wore her hair in a ponytail and her lips were colored pink.

I ain't talkin the dress, goddamnit. I mean the doll. How much fer the doll?

You mean the mannequin? I don't think it's for sale, sir.

Then why yeh got the damn thing in the winder here?

She'd been looking at the floor and now she was looking toward the back of the store.

Can you keep your voice down, please, she said softly.

No I cain't cause yeh ain't hearin me. Jest wantin a answer to my question is all.

Well I don't think it's for sale, sir. I'm sorry.

Well shit then!

The girl was fluttering her eyes about the store like a pair of hummingbird wings.

I could go get my manager? she said. He might be able to help?

Sure's shit hope so. Yeh ain't doin a goddamn thing.

The girl went away and Rigby watched her go. His eyes fell on an old woman staring at him from behind a rack of men's trousers and he cocked his tongue at her and she looked away. The girl was gone a little bit of time and when she came out from the back she was following the manager. He was a tall lanky man with a black mustache. His hair was combed back and he wore a white shirt with a blue tie. His shirtsleeves were rolled to his elbows. He looked at Rigby like one might a vandalized fence. The girl stood behind him like a child would her father.

My name is Gene, the man said. What can I help you with? His voice was low and mirrored his demeanor.

I want a buy this here doll, Rigby said.

I'm sorry it's not for sale.

That's what she told me.

So you know already.

Rigby reached out and rubbed the hard thigh of the mannequin with the back of his hand. Stroked it like a cat.

Don't touch that, Gene said.

Rigby was looking around the store.

Yeh got any black ones? he asked.

That's a black dress there, Gene said.

Dolls I mean. Yeh got any black dolls? That's what I come lookin fer.

The manager smelled the air around Rigby. Have you been drinking, sir?

Naw. I ain't drinkin.

I think you better go.

Hold on now. I ain't tryin to cause nothin.

The manager's face darkened. I said I think you better go. He pointed to the door.

Now hold on, Rigby said.

Betty, Gene said, turning back to the salesgirl, go call Sheriff Fielding.

All right, Rigby said, raising his hands in surrender and pushing past the man. I'm goin.

15

The cruiser pulled to the curb in front of Deb's Café. Stopped a couple of feet away. It was nine o'clock in the morning and the air was thick with heat. A light rain was falling. Sheriff Fielding opened the passenger-side door and looked down into the gutter running with gray water.

Don't worry, Deputy, Fielding said, I'll walk to the curb.

I'll go see what Gene's got to say about this complaint, Clinton said. Then I'll be back. Order me up a couple a eggs won't yeh.

Good enough.

Fielding came in from the rain and stomped the mud from his shoes and shook the water from his collar. He removed his wide hat and said the name of the woman working the counter.

Mornin Sheriff, she said.

He took his regular booth in the back corner and read the

headlines of a paper left behind and set his hat in the center of the table.

A nice, thick woman named Meryl brought the sheriff his coffee in a china mug with a saucer. He smiled warmly at her and ordered the deputy his eggs.

Can I get you anything? she asked.

I guess I wouldn't say no to a muffin.

Bran all right with you?

No blueberry?

Sold my last one to that gentleman there.

Well then I'll take the bran.

He drank the coffee and read the paper. Plucked a cigarette from his breast pocket and lit it. The first drag was long and slow. He finished his coffee and had another. Half an hour passed before he saw the deputy again. By that time it had stopped raining and the deputy's eggs were cold. Fielding was just about to pay when Clinton came through the door and crossed the café in a bit of a hurry and sat down at the booth.

He took off his hat and set it on the table and combed his black hair over with his fingers.

Yer eggs is cold, Fielding said.

Gene said they were robbed last night, Clinton said.

Robbed?

That's what he said.

They get the safe?

Naw. No money was missin.

What the hell they take then?

Clinton grinned.

What's got you amused? Fielding asked.

Some ladies' panties and three brassieres.

Fielding stubbed out his cigarette. Laughed through his nose and shook his head. He tapped the paper with his middle finger as if that would help to explain things.

They found an entire family kilt out in Colorado this week, he said. Whole family murdered for twenty dollars. He frowned and shook. The older I get . . .

Fielding stared at the headline on the paper.

The older yeh get, what sir? Clinton asked.

Fielding laid a dollar on the table.

Nothin. Yeh best eat them eggs. Gene ain't one for patience.

16

Hunting through the woods he heard the voices of girls. Held his breath to make sure. A sharp excitement. Where he looked the tall elms thinned to the river and the gaps there held blades of sunlight and whorls of gnats. In the far distance he could see the limestone bluffs across the water. Great smears of green moss. Shadows mottled the river's surface like cold skin. He was tempted to run. The ferny underbrush stood nearly to his waist as he started toward the noise, leveling his gun.

At a small distance he stood behind a thick oak tree and peeked from around the trunk. In the sandy loam the sun spotlighted three teenage girls taking in the warmth in their bikinis atop beach towels. A small transistor radio stood between them. One girl with blonde hair lay on her stomach with the straps of her top undone and her skin was oiled and brown. The fine hair on her back shone like glitter. Another girl with black hair and freck-led shoulders read aloud from a gossip magazine. Rigby leaned his head against the tree and listened after her voice as though it was only for him. At the funny parts the girls would laugh and Rigby would smile at that.

He watched closely as one girl in a dark blue bikini rose from her towel and stepped into the water. She was a little heavier than the other two, but nicely proportioned with long crimson hair that drifted down to the small of her back. She knelt in the water and lapped up handfuls onto her arms. Had alabaster skin and her heavy breasts hung in the small top. In his mind Rigby imagined this was what Eden might look like. It was a hot day but the water was cool and the girl gave a gasp at its chill. The other girls laughed at her squealing. A little croak of laughter escaped Rigby's lips and all three girls' heads snapped woodward as though on a timer. The girls squinted into the dim forest as if letting their eyes adjust and the girl in the water covered her breasts with an arm.

Hello? the blonde girl said.

A long quiet second passed before Rigby shouldered the shot-gun and lifted his snared rabbit from the forest floor and stepped from behind the tree. The shredded light through the wooded ceiling gave the man a caged appearance like a zoo animal stalking behind the bars. Already he wore a strange grin as he came through the ferns, pushing aside the dogwood and stepping onto the sand. Rigby's dry lips tightened over his long teeth.

What say yeh, he said.

They watched him without a word. The blonde had reached around and begun to tie up the strings of her top.

Don't let me intrude on yeh none, he said, crooked grin. I jest came to say hi yeh.

The blonde girl had sat up and had pulled a shirt around her shoulders. The big-breasted one in the water had come forward and taken up her towel and wrapped it about.

What yeh all doin out here? he asked.

The black-haired girl had her legs curled under. She looked at her friends. Just sun tanning, she said.

Sun tannin? He smiled. That's nice. He tapped his fingers against the barrel of the gun. Well.

They said nothing.

Behind Rigby the woods whistled with the echoes of birds. Downriver, car sounds over the bridge sounded like distant moving water. The blonde girl switched off the radio and then there were only the birds. Rigby sucked through his teeth then spat a gout of foam into the sand. Yeh all alone? he asked.

What do you mean?

Where's yeh all's boyfriends at?

They're coming.

Where they run to?

They didn't run off anywhere, the black-haired girl said.

Yeh all even have boyfriends?

Yeah, said the blonde.

What bout you, he said, pointing the barrel of the shotgun toward the heavier girl.

What about me? she asked.

Yeh got a boy?

Yeah.

No yeh ain't.

You better get out of here before they show up, said the blonde, pretending. She was trying hard to smile. They don't like other guys talking to us, she said. They're jealous.

Jealous?

Mm-hmm.

If they is so jealous they shouldn't leave yeh all by yer lonesome. Rigby swung the dangled rabbit against his leg. He winked at the black-haired girl. Yeh all like rabbit? I could make it up if yeh all is hungry. Build up a nice fire right here. Yeh all want me to make yeh a fire?

We've already eaten lunch, said the black-haired girl.

Rigby's eyes jumped from one to the other. Let them come to rest on the breasts of the redhead and he did not move them for what seemed a long time.

Yeh all could be in them magazines, he said.

What are you talking about?

Not them kind there, Rigby said, pointing to the one laid in front of her. Them other kinds. Them ones fer men to look at.

The blonde cocked her head and scowled at him. That's a disgusting thing to say.

Rigby grinned. He sucked his teeth. Didn't mean it to be.

Well it's rude.

Sorry then.

I'd go if I were you, said the blonde girl, the patience going out of her. They'll be here any minute. They aren't going to like you talking to us the way you are.

I didn't mean nothin. I was jest huntin rabbit and heard yeh all laughin and I thought I'd come see what was so funny.

Well they aren't going to like you being here.

Okay, he said. He allowed himself a good long look at the breasts of the one. Okay, he said again. Don't yeh get a sunburn now. He winked one last time then turned on his heel and retreated into the woods. They heard him go, that thing of the wild, lumbering through the ferns, trodding snapped twigs. And when he was gone they stared at each other with waxed eyes because they didn't know what else to do.

17

It began to rain the next morning. The first stippling over the river. Muted in the woods. Rigby did not leave the boat all day. Busied himself with the tasks of a mouse. When night fell he cooked a supper of pork belly and cut the slab into small pieces and forked each up for the mannequin, Mary Belle. When her rigid face failed to accept the food he threw down the fork and cast the plate to the floor. Stood barking curses at her until he collapsed into the bed. Exhaustion followed his sobbing and then he slept fitfully. He awoke at some point to find her dry wooden eyes staring back in the oil light and he rose like a child from the mattress and took her up like a stuffed toy and dragged her into bed.

In the morning there was a pool of brown water on the countertop from where the roof leaked and the drip stirred him. He went there and eyed up at where the water was falling.

Scratched himself and turned to the bed where Mary Belle had her back turned. He asked her if she was still mad at him but she did not answer.

He brought a chair and climbed up and poked at the sagging patch in the ceiling with a wooden spoon. The vinyl panel tore and a moldy pocket of water fell down upon him. He waved furiously at it and in doing so rocked the legs of the chair out from under him and went crashing to the floor. Pale and naked he looked like some advanced fetus newly birthed writhing balled on the plywood.

Later in the day, in the dying, waxen light he read his magazine to her, what words he could, with her cold face laid into his chest. He'd say, See that? She's got yer same name.

The rain came harder and the daylong the river boiled under the black clouds. The dark sky darkened even further until it was the same color as the river, with Rigby's shadow coming out finally at night to follow him about in the sallow oil lamps like a pup.

18

Rigby climbed the wooden steps in a sway, his head tumbling in drink. On the front of the house there was a porch and no windows in the clapboarding. The white paint was peeling, the porch empty of furniture. Rigby rapped on the door. Two men stood at the far end of the porch smoking cigarettes, regarding him. He looked their way and then he beat the door again. Could hear music within. Stepped back and looked up at the lighted transom and he could see shadow pictures of people playing on the ceiling. He tried the handle but it felt stuck.

There a trick to this? Rigby asked the men down the porch but they didn't offer an answer. He knocked again.

It was a warm night. A big moon rode high in the sky and so bright it turned the land silver. In the open field beyond the house a group of men had built up a bonfire and stood circling it.

Passing a jar and laughing, the pretty flames licking between the opaque figures. The crickets wailed in the tall grass. Nightbirds in the bur oaks. A car had turned off onto the dirt road and began to cut through the trees. It came up into the small parking lot and the headlights caught Rigby's hollow face squinting back at them. Those fiendish lenses catching the light like some deep-sea creature. The men exited the car and said howdy to the guys smoking at the far end. They climbed the steps one at a time.

There some code? Rigby asked.

Code? said one of the men.

Sumpin to git in?

You just walk in, partner.

Door's locked.

I don't think so.

Rigby heard the smoking men chuckle and followed the others inside.

It was an open room with tables arranged over a hardwood floor. There was a bar along one wall with a mirror built into the barback. A raw wood ceiling. Thick beams. A jukebox was playing and girls of all kinds sashayed about to smile at the men and whisper in their ears. Rigby picked out a petite isabelline thing with auburn hair and dull green eyes. Her pouty lips were the color of red cabbage. A black silk slip loose on her shoulders, looking out lazily at the room.

What say darlin? Rigby asked, coming up to her. He was attempting to smooth the cowlick in the back of his head. Wore his cleanest overalls for the occasion and his shirt, which was too big for him, was buttoned to the neck, but still the collar hung like a loose band. He adjusted those comical glasses, flashed his yellow teeth. What's yer name pretty thing?

Why yeh want a know my name?

Thought we'd get friendly first.

I got enough friends.

Yeh got any like me?

Every one a them is like you.

Bet not.

She took stock of him a moment. Against her better judgment she told him.

Caroline, she said.

Like the state?

That's Carolina.

Caroline. That really yer name?

I said it was, didn't I?

Her eyes tracked the length of him. Saw her image dished out in the glass of his lenses.

Yeh lookin to get yerself into somethin tonight or what? she asked. She parted her legs and pulled the hem of her slip up her thighs.

He sat down at the barstool next to her and she reached out for his knee. She leaned in like she had a secret, Rigby trying to look down the neck of her slip. She said, Yeh want a take me in the back, show me what kind a man yeh are?

Why don't yeh give me a little peek, Rigby said.

Yeh got the change?

Yeah. I got money.

Let me see it first.

Jest let me have a peek then I'll show it to yeh.

She sat back abruptly, took her hand from his knee. Yeh sure yeh got the money?

Sure I got it, Rigby said. He'd not taken his gaze from her chest. His big, drunkward eyes. She sighed heavily, then pulled down the front of the slip exposing her peach-colored nipples. Breasts like fruit not quite ripe. When she pulled the fabric up again he said, Let me have another look-see.

Yeh ain't gettin anothern less yeh take me in the back. Shoot, yer already in a little now.

All right then.

She led him by the hand to the back room. Along the way he heard the moans of women behind closed doors. The narrow hallway was pitched in red lighting and lanky girls leaned smoking against the walls with their robes fallen open like addicts. The room she took him to was plain looking: only a bed, a mirror, and a basin of water and a hand towel pegged to the wall. A cheap lamp with some dangling fringe burning beside the basin was the only light. She went to the basin and took down the towel and dabbed a corner into the water and reached it up under her slip and cleaned herself. The muffled grind of bedsprings came through the walls. She hung the towel back on the wall and turned to him.

It's five dollers to blow yeh, she said. Ten if yeh want a fuck me. And twenty if yeh want it any other way. She crossed the room and looped her arms around his neck like she'd always been his sweetheart. So what sounds good, honey?

Blushing a little he said, That all sounds good.

She reached down. Rigby was already hard.

I can give yeh a half hour for twenty-five and yeh can have anythin yeh want.

Like a sale yer runnin on yerself, Rigby said with a grin. That include this?

He tapped her buttocks like a drum.

Long as yeh don't go over half a hour you can have me anyway yeh want.

Okay, I'll take that then. Rigby went to kiss her but she shied.

Got a pay first, she said. She let go of him and slipped the straps from her shoulders and the slip piled at her feet like snow.

Yeh can put the money on the table there, she said.

Her fingers began to work at his zipper. Groping him as she did it.

Let me give it to yeh when we're done, Rigby said. His eyes were closed.

She stopped and took a step back. Yeh ain't got it, have yeh?

Sure I got it.

No yeh ain't.

Let me owe it to yeh.

She lifted her slip from the floor and went to the door. She leaned out and called for someone named Jimmy.

I got it, said Rigby. I jest have to owe it to yeh is all.

She stood back and crossed her arms as a big man entered the room.

Come on, said the man.

I told her I'm good fer it.

Come on, he said again.

As Rigby passed the girl he hissed, Yeh ain't nothin but a shitty hognosed whore.

In an instant the man whipped him across the face and Rigby fell to the floor. Balled up like a turtle. His lip split like a plum. The man kicked him once with his boot then dragged him out of the room by the straps of his overalls and through the barroom and flung him outside. The men smoking were still there on the porch and they laughed as Rigby groaned in the dirt under the moon, clutching his ribs. Then once and then twice, the blue moonlight winked in the dished lens of the glasses as the bouncer tossed them into the darkness behind Rigby, leaving him to paw blindly around in the mud like a vole.

19

In his dwelling malaise. Propped crookedly in a rickety aluminum chair in the already dank heat of the morning, poisoning
himself with whiskey. He sat cross-legged the way old men do
and glared through a bludgeoned eyesocket. A heron at the bank
stepped mechanically among the blue shade of the far shore. The
river sounded like a sigh.

He'd awoken alone in his bed. No recollection of how he had
come to be there or who or what might have lent a hand. Then
came fractured memories. Awoke with his shoes still on. His shirt
was torn and crimson-colored at the collar. A large oxblood stain
was dried into his trouser leg. He smelled of urine. Awoke when
the sun bled through the thin curtains and he rose slowly in a
spew of curses like another kind of Lazarus. He ran his dry cat's
tongue over his split lip, wincing as the cut opened again. He

found a small tin of aspirin under the sink but that was empty save a fine powder in the bottom. Tilted the tin over his mouth and tapped the bottom.

On deck, drinking his rye, peace did not find him. His temples pounded like drums and his ears wailed. Stewing there, unwilling to move, the sun broke from the limestone hills, flooding the shadowed places, spilling over the river. The woods hushed with this sudden awakening as though all manner of creature paused in awe for a moment. There were no clouds in that sky and there was no wind. Rigby stood painfully from his chair and knelt with more than a little effort to the warped boards of the deck and he laid the good side of his face against it. Watched the water and the heron hunting and then he closed his eyes.

He did not wake or move save for once when he was roused by the passing of a small fishing boat. The smoky outboard clattering off the bluffs, and to this Rigby edged on his belly to the deck's gunwale and pulled himself out and pissed into the slough, neither holding it nor watching. When he was done he rolled to a place in the shade, not fastening his overalls, and called to Mary Belle for a glass of water. And then he closed his eyes again.

WITNESS #6

No one saw him for a long while. Betty and Gene weren't the only ones who claimed he'd taken lady things. Let me see, there was Dick and Joan down at Stimpson's Pharmacy on the other side of town, and Agnes Filson, she worked the cosmetics department at J. C. Penney. She said he came in one day asking about eyeshadow. She didn't know if he took anything, but she said, and I agree, it would've been awful peculiar to see a man like Rigby in the cosmetics department just looking around. I don't know if that helps any. And shoot, look at me, where are my manners. Would you like some coffee?

20

Coming down the higher reaches of the valley the road swung through the tall elms and cut lower like a knife slice in the hill. It had not rained in some time and the dirt road was dusty and the risen dust of passing cars powdered the long ditch grass like snow. Rigby walking under a white-hot sun with his paper bag of treasures and the broken bill of his cap pulled low. Watching that slice of road across the river he saw a belch of dust rise from the trees like steam from a train. He lost it when the road slipped between a draw of limestone. Then he saw a car cross the bridge. He adjusted the sack in his arms and hurried on.

The sun was just past noon when the dull growl of an engine piqued Rigby's ears. He didn't turn to see it, just stepped closer to the narrow shoulder and kept on. The car slowed as it came up behind him then slowed to his pace. Heard the passenger window unroll and then he saw the polished wheel panel of the police cruiser.

What say yeh, Rigby? Sheriff Fielding had his elbow resting in the window. Yeh headin home?

Yep, Rigby said quickly, not stopping.

What yeh got there in that sack?

Nothin.

Why don't you stop walkin a second and we can talk some.

I got supper on, Rigby said.

Supper? said Fielding. Why it's only a little after noon. Yeh stewin somethin?

Yeah.

What yeh got stewin?

Nothin. Jest some rabbit.

I see. Well why don't yeh hold up there a second and we can chat some.

Fielding said something to the deputy and the deputy pulled in front of Rigby and parked the car. Rigby was forced to stop. Watched the sheriff step from the cruiser and pull up on his belt. Fielding squared his hat and spit into the ditch. The deputy had joined the sheriff near the trunk of the car. Fielding pointed to the paper bag in Rigby's arms.

Fixins for the rabbit? he asked.

Fer the what?

The stew. Get yourself some onions and carrots to put in with the rabbit?

Oh, said Rigby. Yeah. Fixins.

Mind if I have a look?

Jest taters and onions like yeh said.

Naw, I said carrots. Let me have a look. The deputy here can make sure I don't steal nothin.

Give him a look, said Clinton.

I got a git on, Rigby said, muttering. Got a rabbit stewin. Got a git on.

He'd tried to sneak between the sheriff and the deputy but the sheriff had held out his hand and snatched the sack from Rigby.

Looky here, said Fielding. Inside was a box of pantyhose and some red lipstick. Now this don't look like onions or carrots. He held the bag open for Clinton to see. Clinton reached in and poked at each item.

Fielding said, Deputy, you see any onions or carrots under them pantyhose?

No I don't, Sheriff.

Neither do I. Rigby, what're yeh doin with pantyhose and lipstick? You got a girl you're seein?

The lawmen laughed.

Rigby watched the road at his feet, the shadows there. His closed mouth moved like he was chewing a piece of fat.

Gene, said Fielding, down at Wilson's, he said he saw yeh take some things without payin for em. Is that what happened? I'd hate to think Gene was lyin to me.

There was a pause. A redwing blackbird called in the bushes and they could hear frogs down by the river. Rigby shifted on his feet and Clinton spat onto the road.

I tell yeh what, Fielding said. Just let me see the receipt for these here things and you can get on your way back to that stew a yours.

When Rigby didn't move Fielding said, Well you better come on with us, Rigby. Get this straightened out.

21

The county clerk recorded the indictment, charged Rigby with shoplifting. Other charges followed. Gene also filed for public intoxication and disturbing the peace. The woman whose boy Rigby had tripped wanted assault and battery to a minor thrown in too. He was not indicted for those crimes but to appease certain citizens of Oscar, Rigby was laid away in a cell in the Allamakee County jailhouse.

Five days and nights he lay about on the stiff bed counting the cracks in the plastered ceiling. A parade of drunks came and went. One early morning a man screamed about a rat. There was singing at night down the concrete corridor and Rigby pressed the thin pillow they'd given him over his ears and thought about Mary Belle.

The first night he slept with his head to the bars and was

woken by the errant spackling of piss against his face as the man across the hall peed through the bars at him. On the third day they led him out into the yard to air. It was raining and he stood hunkered against the wall in what little dry space there was, holding his collar closed tight against his chin. He asked the guard for a cigarette but the guard said he didn't smoke. Supper each night was beans and cabbage.

On the third night he was woken by the man in the next cell over, telling him to quit his blubbering.

The man said, Quit goin on bout her.

I ain't goin on bout anybody, Rigby hissed. Leave me be.

He rolled to his side, facing the wall. Thought it was all done.

A small period of time, and the man said, Who's Lila DeWitt?

In the yard the next day, under a white-hot sun, the man in the next cell found him, said, You the one blubberin bout yer mam last night?

Rigby craned his neck to see his interrogator. Was squatted on his hams, held his hand like a visor. The man stood directly in front of the sun and the light nimbused his head.

Are yeh? the man asked.

I ain't got no mama, Rigby said.

No yeh ain't, the man said. Because she dead. Ain't a DeWitt no more neither. Died a Hobson.

Still squatted there, plucking brown grass, Rigby listened as the man told him what he knew. When he was finished Rigby said,

Why yeh tellin me this?

The man shrugged. Cause yeh was cryin bout her.

I think yer lyin a me.

Again, the man shrugged.

Alright, he said. See yeh round.

On the fifth day he was released. Sheriff Fielding told him to quit stealing. It was raining that day and by the time he walked the five miles to the houseboat he was soaked through and his heels in the soggy brogans had blistered. Mary Belle was seated at the table where he'd left her. And seeing her face, and what he took for disappointment, he ran to the mattress and clapped his hands over the back of his head and wailed like a hound into his pillow.

22

A false fall arrived at the end of August that year. A gray sky with a cold wind. The houseboat pulled in new directions and there were new sounds to get used to. Morning had the smell of colder weather, geese honking and congregating in parking lots. Thoughts of his mother swirling like eddies.

Rigby kept out of sight. Walked to town only when his cupboards thinned, and even then he spoke to no one. Picking through the stocked shelves of the nearest store. Yellow cheese and tins of Vienna sausages and sardines, bundling those in his arms and spilling them over the counter beside the till. The thin cashier in a white apron tallied up the goods and eyed him with suspicion.

End of summer, said the man, bagging the groceries.

Mmm, said Rigby. He was picking at the corner of the counter where the formica was lifting.

Don't pick at that.

Rigby levered up his eyes to the man.

Dollar forty, the cashier said.

Dry of drink nearly the whole of August, he stumbled upon a canvas bag holding three bottles on the steps of a gas station. He raced away with his prize, clambering into a ditch and just into the woods where he uncorked the first bottle and drank a quarter of it. That night he danced. Swayed with Mary Belle in his arms, humming some out-of-tune number. The north wind blew.

Winter came too soon. The ice hung like chandeliers in the forest and winds set the trees heeling and crackling like fire. The weather brought a freeze to the slough. The houseboat locked in time. See him during those short days gathering sticks, piles of moss, disks of frozen shit and hauling them cradled in his arms to burn in his stove. Mary Belle seemed to eye him with contempt like she deserved better. Some nights he'd wake to her staring blankly at him from her tilted place in the floor as though she was capable of judgment.

Christmas came with falling snow. Lighted trees in all the town windows. Wreaths hung on doors and cedar garland snaked like vines in storefronts. Carols being played everywhere. Christmas Eve he listened on an AM station to the nativity broadcast. Mary and Joseph in the manger. The birth of Jesus. The tinny voices of the radio actors sounding far off through the little speaker. He had cooked a Christmas supper of baked beans and sardines. He crouched near the stove, eating his paltry meal with his eyes closed, imagining what Bethlehem might look like.

He'd not thought of his mother in quite a while but the tinsel revelry of the season made him feel something like nostalgia. *Something like nostalgia* because he'd never seen her face save the fleeting hours his clouded infant eyes gazed at her before she left him. Never heard her voice, the way it might sound when she said his name. *Something like nostalgia* because all he had of her was his own invention. And when the seasons warmed again he resolved to amend that.

With the advent of 1960 came the cold. Second week of the New Year, colder yet, found Rigby huddled before the stove. Pulled his mattress over the floor. Wrapped in his blankets in the pallid light he looked like a stone figurine. A gothic monk vowed to a different penance.

It began to snow one morning. Didn't let up for a week straight. He'd shovel the deck with a discarded license plate he'd found on the roadside, gouging a narrow footpath into the drifts. Then his bootpack leading up the bank where it scattered like the tracks of animals come and gone in the night. Near the thirtieth of January the clouds broke. First time all month. The stars appeared, a moon like a silver dollar. He stumbled onto the deck and howled at the glimmering sky.

A bright day in February. Set about in the woods with his shotgun hunting up whatever might be out there, he heard the voices of two boys. He was trespassing on private land and the sound of them sent Rigby to his belly in the snow. The boys on a road at the forest's edge. A white field beyond. A few brittle cornstalks stood through the snow to tremble in the wind. Each boy carried a small-caliber rifle slung across the back in the fashion of a bandolier. They looked like brothers. The bigger one carried a limp rabbit over his shoulder. Rigby laid the barrel of his gun on a felled log and trained his sight on the smaller one. He gauged the wind and led the boy at five feet. The boys were talking excitedly about something, but Rigby couldn't hear what exactly. With his thumb he pushed off the safety and his forefinger tickled the trigger. He trained the sight for the younger one's head and then whispered, Bang. The boys rounded a bend in the road and fell from view, and with the safety still off Rigby retreated into the woods.

23

Spring brought a thaw. The ice thinned and gave up its hold on the slough. Artifacts of winter began to unearth with the melting snow. Months of shit and garbage, memories of cold. Cans and bottles and bones. A junkheap where crows came to pick over the scraps and squawk at each other.

The tree blossoms flowered and for a few days the air was clean and sweet smelling. Then, as it does, a strong wind came and blew all of those flowers away. A cold rain, and all the white and pink petals lay sodden over the ground. Then there was nothing in the air but the humus odor of the slough so thick you could almost chew it.

When the rains would quit he'd oar his skiff out to run his lines in the eddy where the current of the river flushed past the slough. He'd set three lines to anchored floats, each with a string of barbed hooks baited with scraps of offal. Midday he'd check in on the lines, evening he'd haul them in. He enjoyed the taste of catfish, and in that coppered hour before twilight he'd clean them on the bank, saving the guts in a bucket for the next day and slipping the pink fillets into a pail of water.

He'd found another mannequin over the winter in a dumpster behind a factory. Had taken her home and introduced her to Mary Belle. He'd pulled out his charred magazine, folded and creased, his favorite pages dog-eared. Thumbed through it till he found a pretty brunette posed near a fireplace, nothing but black panties and an unbuttoned white cardigan sweater. The new mannequin's shape wasn't exactly the same but Rigby didn't mind. The pinup's name was Suzy Lee and Rigby liked that name very much.

At first he was worried they wouldn't get along. He'd set the table and then sat them there with their stiff necks twisted, face to face, as to get to know one another. Rigby stood back with his arms folded over his chest, watching them in the soft oil light. Waiting for who knows what. It was snowing that first night and he could hear the wind in the flue. After some time he held his hands up, said, Okay. I ain't goin to force it. Yeh take yer time.

That was three months ago, and by Rigby's judgment the three of them had become very close.

Rowing back, he craned his head. He had caught one big catfish and it wormed in the shallow bilge of the skiff. Its wide mouth opened and closed as it sucked at the tarry air. There was no wind and no sound save for the wheeze of the wooden oars in their locks. Up the slough Rigby eased his oaring and watched the roiling water behind the transom. The marks where the oar blades dimpled the scum. He watched a kingfisher go ratcheting from a gray tree limb. He saw a muskrat paddling slowly along the shoreline. Close to home he spun the skiff abeam to the houseboat and shipped the oars and sat there watching the image within the window, like a husband might pulling into his driveway. At the sink stood Mary Belle and Suzy Lee with their carmine smiles glossed on. Hands he'd set in gestures of welcome.

WITNESS #7

Hell, I might a told him about it for all I know. Heard him blabbin on bout a lady named DeWitt. Said it in his sleep. I was in there with him. Yeh jest hear things is all. Jailhouse in a county like that ain't big. Hear all kind a things. Anyways, says it in his sleep one night. I said to him the next day, said, Say partner, I know who DeWitt is. Lila DeWitt. I said, Who she to you? Could tell by the look on his face it was his mama. Anyways, told him my brother was neighbors with her down in Cedar Rapids. Except now she wasn't a DeWitt. She was a Hobson. Told him, Partner I got bad news. So what I tell him is his mama married and had two other kids. Told him, she's dead. Moren fifteen years back. Went on to say they made a big stink bout it in the papers. Real tragedy. Her car went off a bridge, two babies in the back seat. That last part, the babies part, that seemed to upset him. Don't know if he was cryin or snarlin.

24

The full moon had crested the canopy of trees and flooded the graveyard in an aluminum light. Each headstone threw a spectral shadow over the wet grass. Many were coated in lichen. Some of the nicer ones, carved in marble, were polished and stood gleaming in the night, catching the light of the moon and winking it back so brightly that when Rigby closed his eyes he saw hundreds of moons burned into his eyelids. The crickets out there quit at his coming and commenced again behind him. At one point he climbed atop a headstone and turned back and saw his footprints in the dew vanish like a ghost returning to the grave. He felt like a phantom and to anyone caring to listen said, Boo.

The day before he had hitched to Cedar Rapids. A trucker with a mean dog kicked him out about an hour north of the city. Sellers asked him if he liked to put peanut butter on his genitals and let the dog lick it off. Not the first time Rigby had had a gun pulled on him.

He found the cemetery in the late afternoon. He walked among the headstones, trying to read the names. The grounds were well tended to and over some of the graves flowers lay on the grass. The cemetery was nearly empty, only a single couple with a small child at the far end, the boy racing to catch grasshoppers.

Then there it was. Thirty years, almost an incantation. A name only rumored over. Four syllables murmured in his dreams. A name that made him think of flowers. He knelt to make sure. He ran his bony fingertip over the stone. Traced out each letter, but did not say her name. An epitaph read:

LILA HOBSON.

LOVING WIFE, MOTHER, DAUGHTER.

The names of her new children, Jacob and Patrick, written below.

At sunset a groundskeeper shooed him away, and standing on the pavement just without, Rigby watched the big steel gates swing closed, the young groundskeeper eyeing him oddly as he snapped shut the lock, turning once to look back at this strange visitor before he got in his truck and drove off.

Sellers waited for a long time. Hiding in the bushes outside of the cemetery, he lounged like an emaciated climber in a tent waiting for better weather. He'd brought some tins of sardines, and he ate them slowly, savoring one at a time. He was giddy. He had broken into the toolshed well after the moon had come up

and taken a spade that he now lay beside with the kind of pride a
soldier might his rifle.

The spade sank easily into the dirt. The grass was soft from wa-
tering and the dew. He worked himself into a lather and stripped
out of his clothes so that he was digging in only a pair of soiled
drawers. It was a ridiculous sight. His thin arms and ribcage
flashing under the skin, he looked like some kind of wobbling
stork flailing about in the dirt. But he was singing, or something
like it, quietly as he went about this quixotic task. Lower and
lower. First to his knees, and then his waist disappearing, his
shoulders, till finally he was only a head clucking just above the
ground.

At two in the morning the spade struck something hollow.
Rigby's heart jumped. He stabbed down again, as if he didn't believe it. This time the point of the spade stabbed into the wood
and stuck there. He dislodged the shovel and began to scrape the
coffin but, quickly losing his patience and falling to his knees, tore
at the clods of dirt with his hands. The coffin was dark with dirt
and stain, but where his spade had pierced the surface the wood
was like the meat of an apple.

It didn't take long to uncover the lid of the coffin, but all of
his excitement and all of his anxiety were halted by a sharp grip
of fear. His own shadow under the moon was supine over the lid
and for a minute, however briefly, it was he in the coffin and not
his mother.

Why'd yeh leave me? he asked plainly.

With more than a little effort he heaved the heavy lid from the box and what he found sent him reeling on his heels to collapse in the dirt alongside the coffin.

His mother was almost a skeleton. A little hair, which never goes away, on her head. She was dressed in a formal outfit with a dress reaching her ankles and the sleeves running to her wrists. Nearly bone as she was, the dress looked like shed snake skin. What horrified him most was not the macabre image of his mother, but the bones of two children she held in her arms in an eternal embrace.

One must have been no more than three years old. The other just an infant. The infant was in a baptismal gown and the bigger one in knickers and tiny saddle shoes. Both of their heads were turned so they were gazing eyeless at each other, with their cheeks resting against their mother's bosom. Death or not, the sight was one of compassion and love, and that his mother, who had abandoned him so long ago, could have the agency to love these boys as she had not loved him, sent him into a rage.

He ripped each child from her arms and cast them from the grave. With nothing holding them intact save their frail clothing, the bones separated and the pieces were scattered. There was venom in his breath. He cursed the tiny bones to hell. Who knows how long it went on for. When it was over he crumpled atop his mother and wept over the ribs where there had once been a heart.

The houseboat was dark when he arrived home the following day. He came in with a rucksack on his shoulder. Mary Belle and Suzy Lee were seated at the table. In the bent moonlight struggling through the greasy panes, the dolls could almost be seen.

Nothing moved. No sound and no movement anywhere. Not a
whisper of wind and even the houseboat seemed to be held in
place as if by some giant hand. Rigby crossed the room and lit the
oil lamp. The details of the dolls' gaudy faces grew with the light.
The bowls of whatever slop he had fixed them gone cold and hard.

He set the pack on the warped floor and went to the sink and
poured a long drink of some burning astringent into a chipped
mug. Drank that and poured another. Then he went back to the
pack in the floor and lugged it to the table. He opened the top
carefully, pulling a single piece of rope. He tilted it for the dolls
to see.

I want yeh to meet yer mothernlaw, he said.

Heaped in a pile were the bones of Lila Hobson. The skull
with its grotesque strands of hair was staring upward into the
condemned light.

Don't worry girls, he said, yer nuttin like her.

That night after he had laid the dolls in his bed he pulled
up the plywood floor and dumped in his mother's remains. In
the malarial light of the oil lamp, he spent the next several hours
piecing together the bones, arranging them into a picture of tran-
quil repose. When they looked the way he thought they should,
he stood over her for a moment and realized he had no memory
of her and that this was to be the indelible image of a woman
he knew nothing about. Without a word, he stepped from the
shallow bilge, looked at his mother a final time, and then ham-
mered back into place the rotten plywood floor that had become
her crypt.

25

One day he found a baby doll floating near the main stream of the river after running his lines. The doll was floating face up, its small plastic fingers reaching from the water. Its eyes were the kind that closed when the doll was laid on its back but the doll was old and appeared to have been in the river for quite some time. The lids were stuck open by river grime and any color that might have personalized the doll was gone so that it stared blankly through black glass eyes.

He rowed over and took it by the hand and lifted it gently from the water, setting it in the floor of the skiff alongside a string of bass. He floated for a few minutes with the oars shipped as he stared into the dark eyes. He smiled finally, and reached down and with a hooked finger tickled the doll's belly. Waggled the little toe of one of the little feet. Then he took a bandana from his pocket and dipped it in the water and wiped the scum that browned its legs, its chest. He folded the bandana again and dabbed at the scum ring that haloed the thing's face. One of the bass kicked its tail and the slimy fin slapped the baby's neck. Rigby lashed out at the fish with his knife and then hurled it, stringer and all, into the water. The boat still, he removed his shirt and wadded it beneath the doll so it might serve as a bed.

When he got home he dallied the line at the deck and crawled out of the boat, then leaned in and lifted the baby in his arms as if he'd just returned home from the hospital. He walked proudly into the house with the baby wrapped in his shirt, said, Mary Belle, looky what I found fer yeh.

He set the baby on the table and then made Mary Belle's arms into a cradle. Lifted it into her arms. He stepped back and for a moment he felt very moved, and nearly crying, said, Yeh'll be a good mama. Then he said, Don't worry yerself there Suzy Lee, I'll find yeh one too.

Again, he thought of his mother. Nagging him like a toothache.

26

He looked for it to rain. The clouds had that look. Cotton balls dipped in black ink and laid across the sky. He leaned from the deck to look up at them. Thought he heard the long roll of distant thunder but perhaps that was only in his mind. The day grew hot and windless. The trees across the slough stood bearded in haze. He watched a couple of mallards kick in the current and he laughed at them as they stepped out of the tea-colored water and shook their tail curls.

A little after noon he heard voices. Stood suddenly with his hand cupped at his ear. Rigby looked at the woods downriver as though they authored the noise. Soon the bow of a metal canoe speared around the bend oared by a teenage couple. He dashed from the deck into a thicket of catbrier along the bank where he gripped the thorny branches, parting a spyhole. The couple was talking excitedly about whatever but the voices fell away as the canoe neared the houseboat. The boy in the aft dug in his paddle and the canoe swung as far opposite as the slough would allow. Rigby watched warily through the tangle of vine as both boy and girl turned to regard the floating bit of waste they skirted. Eyes like dinner plates and their paddles scooping as quietly as they could. Rigby spied camping gear stowed between them. A Styrofoam cooler. Fishing poles. The boy craned his neck a final time as the houseboat receded back into the pall. Out of view Rigby heard the girl laugh as a defense against fear and he cursed them, gibbering like some simian thing stooped there in the brush.

27

Stalking through the warm nightwoods the campfire came into view like another kind of sun. They'd pitched their tent in a small opening of elm trees the color of bone. The fire was built against the opening of a limestone combe and the smoke blackened the rock. Rigby had expected a scene of repose; what he saw instead drove him headlong to hunker in the scrub and clasp his hand over his mouth. On a blanket near the fire the girl rode atop the boy with naked hips. She was bronzed in the firelight and her small gilded breasts hardly moved. The echoing sounds Rigby heard were a kind of litany. He watched her clever hips and felt a rousing. The boy held tightly onto the girl's thighs and with their eyes closed both were lost to the world.

Rigby laid his shotgun by and unfastened his trousers. He watched from that elevated vantage like God down upon Eden.

She said the name Billy. She said it again, and in a whisper Rigby said, Now say mine. He knelt there watching them until it was over.

She'd hung her clothes on a tree limb and for the next hour went about her jobs just as God had made her. Cooking supper and cleaning the dishes. Her nipples gold with firelight, a little hair between her legs. She tempted the boy with a swim and dove hands first into the slough. The moon broke all over the surface like pouring embers, and Rigby watched the sparkle of all that dim light on the water. She came rearing from the surface, her hair slick and the stars panned over her skin. She swam about for a while, calling Billy's name.

Rigby lay out till the fire was nearly gone, a dull pulse of ember. Confident now of the snores he heard, he gathered up the gun and crawled to the edge of the camp. He tiptoed over the sand. Next to the Styrofoam cooler he crouched with the gun cradled in his lap and stared a long time at the zippered flap of the tent. Cicadas started up in the trees like small sirens. A mosquito gnashed in his ear. He stood and found the girl's bikini limp on a tree branch and sniffed it. Stuffed that into his trousers. He turned and eyed the tent again. What little light offered by the glowing embers painted the tent with his shadow and that shadow grew as he came up on it.

He knelt at the flap and with the barrel of the shotgun pulled the thin nylon back. His heart trembled and quaked, his hands like they'd taken a chill, as the shapes of their bodies

accrued out of the darkness. He looked at the boy first, his back
to him. Then he looked at the girl. Only a sheet covered her and
he allowed his eyes to linger on the warm curve of her hip. Figured there must be more. So he reached to part the sheet from
her breast thinking he might steal a glimpse. But at the first slip
of the sheet the girl's eyes snapped open and seeing this impish
troll above her she screamed horribly. The sudden start threw
Rigby backpedaling into the dirt where he lost his hold on the
shotgun. Left him sprawled on his back on the ground. Heard
the booming of the boy's voice, the girl wailing. He scrambled,
raking the dirt and twigs where the gun had fled. His scraping
nails had just reached the wooden stock when a hand clamped
around his ankle.

You son of a bitch, Rigby heard the boy say.

All too quick Rigby rolled and levered back the hammer and
shot the boy through the chest. The shot pitched him back like
he was a carnival target jerked on its string. The tent crumpled
under the weight of him as he fell and he lay there bleeding out as
the girl kicked and reeled from within. The report of the gunblast
was incredibly loud against the limestone wall, and the ringing in
Rigby's ears drowned out the girl's screams.

Rigby had gotten himself to his feet and stood shivering over
the dying boy. The ragged opening was black and slick as oil. The
boy sucked down air only for it to escape gurgling through his
chest. There were words writ in those troubled young eyes but
he spoke none of them and then he died. Rigby levered back the
second hammer and leveled the barrel at the writhing girl within
the tent. He could make out the shape of her head and he took

aim. His finger pressured the trigger. But just as he was about to pull it he let the gun slip from his shoulder and trained the barrel toward the sky and fired at the stars. She gave out another burst of horror as Rigby raced into the woods.

28

John and Ruth Halverson were coming home from a church social that night. Just a little gathering and because the social was held in the church's basement and because of the kind of people the Halversons were all they had had to drink that night was fruit punch.

It was a clear night and warm and the moon was full and the trees and the fields and the river were all silver under it. Out John's window were the tall elms standing against the river and out Ruth's were the fields. Out over the fields was a thin fog like lace and like tiny gunfire within the thin fog were hundreds of lightning bugs. It was late and Ruth commented on it: Been years since we've been out this late.

Goin a pay hell in the mornin, John said.

You watch your mouth, John Halverson, she said.

The old truck pittered down the dirt road. Ruth leaned to turn on the radio. Began fiddling with the knob. John leaned over the wheel and looked up at the sky.

Thought it might rain tonight, he said. Look at all them stars.

He rolled down his window and put his elbow there. The air was thick and sweet and smelled like moss and limestone and slow-moving water. The frogs were wailing down near the mud and the crickets were trying to keep up. Ruth was going back and forth across the bandwidth and John said: Cain't yeh jest settle on somethin already?

I want to find something romantic, John. Maybe we could pull over and do some dancing under the stars.

He did not answer but he smiled and that settled it.

The road made a bend down the way at one of the sloughs and when they got there John slowed the truck and the headlights washed across the pale trunks of the trees and the green grass of the ditch and then back to the dirt road and before he could shift gears the naked girl came into view and John slammed on the brakes. Ruth was still looking down at the radio.

Ruth, he said.

From the radio came a Glenn Miller song. She looked up at him.

John, what are you doing?

Ruth.

Like his eyes were tethered to something out there, she followed his gaze.

Oh my God, she said.

The girl looked like a ghost standing in the road. Her skin

was colorless in the headlights. Her hair was hanging down over her face and wet-looking. Her arms were folded up over her chest.

That's one a them Dahl girls, John said. Ain't it?

That's Hannah, Ruth said.

John reached behind the seat and took up a blanket.

Here, he said. Go get her. She'll know yer voice.

Ruth opened her door carefully as if to not scare away a wild animal. She called her name. The dome light lit up the cab and John held his hand like a visor. Ruth said the girl's name again. Hannah turned, and like a deer, took off in the opposite direction. Ruth followed after her, calling her name, and with the passenger door still open John popped the clutch and killed the engine and said, Goddamnit!

He turned the key and the engine turned over and over and finally caught and he ground the transmission into gear and chased on after them.

It was a quarter mile down the road before the two of them came into sight. They were seated in the road, right there on the dirt. Ruth had the girl in her lap, wrapped in the blanket, rocking her like an infant. John stopped the truck and got out and stood there looking at his wife who was looking at him and nothing was said and it was completely still except for the wailing frogs and the Glenn Miller and the quiet roar of the slow-moving river.

29

Deputy Clinton rapped on the storm screen of Fielding's house and wiped his feet on the mat. He stood back and put his hands on his belt and looked off into the dark yard. He was a slender, punctual man in his late twenties who seemed to garner his worth by making the sheriff proud. A big moon and all the stars held the night sky and the land was shadowed by all that light. Fielding's wife, Sara, answered the door in her housedress and said good evening to the deputy with a certain amount of worry in her eyes. He took off his hat and looked into the house. She must have known the reason for his late visit was bad for a deathly pallor drew down her face like a piece of pale fabric and her hand slipped from the door handle.

I'll get Amos, she said.

They drove to the courthouse and Clinton told him what he

knew. The courthouse was empty and there wasn't but one truck in the parking lot. They climbed the granite steps and Clinton held the door for the sheriff. Their shoes over the hard floor echoed down the vacant halls. Where Fielding's office was they saw his secretary standing in the doorway. When she saw them a look of relief fell over her like water.

Sitting in the office was an older couple and a girl wrapped in a wool blanket. The woman had her arm around the girl. When Fielding entered the office the man stood and shook his hand.

John, said the sheriff, nodding.

Sheriff.

Fielding put his hand on the woman's shoulder as he took a seat on the corner of his desk. The deputy stood off to the side and hooked his thumbs in his belt. Fielding took off his hat and set it gently on the desk as if a baby were asleep in the room. He looked down at the girl and didn't know what to say at all. She was trembling like a cold dog. Had cuts all down her arms and legs like she'd been rolled in brier thorns. Maybe she had. The girl was shoeless and her feet were caked in dried mud.

Bets, Fielding said to his secretary, go find her some clothes will yeh?

The woman seated beside the girl started to stand. I'll go with you, she said.

No, Ruth, said Fielding, you stay. I need to know what's goin on here. He looked at the girl. Spoke softly. Yer name's Hannah, ain't it? The girl didn't answer. Fielding said, Can you tell me what happened?

The girl's blue eyes were glossy as though drunk, though she wasn't, and she rocked like a metronome in her chair. Ruth tucked a tangle of blonde hair behind her ear. There was a purple smudge drifting toward her jaw and her bottom lip was split and crusted in black blood. Fielding nodded Clinton to a pitcher of water on a narrow table along the wall.

Seth, he said, will you get her a glass a water?

The deputy brought the glass of water and Ruth held it to the girl's dry lips. She attempted a drink off it but the water spilled down her chin onto her lap and she began to cry.

Fielding looked at his deputy. Why don't you go find Bets.

An hour slipped away before the girl said anything. John and Fielding had stepped out into the hall and John told him what he'd seen.

Where'd her clothes go? Fielding asked.

Like I told yeh. I don't know. Just found her there like that.

Hmm, Fielding said with his arms crossed. Looked into the office. She's one a them Dahl girls ain't she?

Yeah, John said.

I better call her parents.

By the time she stopped trembling it was well past midnight. Her mother and father arrived, held her between them. In the shapeless clothes Betsy had found she started in slowly. Had to take breaks and hold her face in her hands. The girl told them about the camping, the place up the slough. Then she told them about the man outside the tent. As she spilled the wicked details Betsy brought her hand to her mouth.

Did yeh see his face? Fielding asked.

The girl tried to describe it. It was dark, she said.

Did he do anything to yeh? He violate yeh in any way?

No, she said. Her little voice like a brittle leaf about to come off a tree.

Yeh sure? Fielding asked.

She nodded.

And if we were to go look, would your boyfriend still be there?

The girl began to cry suddenly and her mother pulled her into her arms. The sheriff bowed his head and sighed. Go round up some flashlights, Seth. John, you want a show us where yeh found her?

All right.

Fielding took another long look at the girl but whatever words were forming stayed that way and he knew all the thinking he'd done in his lifetime and all the things he thought he had an answer to didn't total to anything. Seth came through the door with the flashlights clutched in his hands.

Yeh ready? he asked.

30

They drove out of town, out the dirt road where John and Ruth had first seen her. Wash of yellow headlights flooding the ditches, a mouse or two skittering across the road, John sitting in the back of the cruiser not saying anything until the spot where Hannah had stood naked and trembling, then said, Here we are.

Pull over, Seth, Fielding said.

In the darkness Fielding stood with his hands on his belt looking into the dark woods, up at the sky broken by stars. He stepped away from the cruiser and into the headlights. Turned where he stood, gazing at the ground as if searching for something. Then he knelt and picked up a rock, examined it, let it fall, and then looked off down the dark road for a moment.

Back in the cruiser, said, This ain't far from Sellers's place, is it?

Nope, Clinton said.

Well.

They turned off where a narrow dirt road led to the head of the slough. Drove as far as they could. Their flashlights traversed the dark woods like satellites in another sky. The strange shadows seemed to shift of their own volition. There were nightbirds and the frogs in the distance.

The deputy followed Fielding with a shotgun laid on his shoulder, barrel skyward, his finger just outside of the trigger guard. A thin fog hung near the floor of the woods and the sheriff's flashlight bored a dim shaft like the headlamp of some diminished train. It was a half-mile walk to the slough and they didn't say a word. The snapping of a stick came like a shot fired from the woods beyond and the sheriff stopped and cocked his head in that direction. The deputy seemed to hold his breath. Fielding swung the flashlight into that barred view of pale trunks and a pair of red eyes burned back at him.

Jesus, said Clinton with a start. Then shook his head at the doe standing there. Bout give me a heart attack.

The doe stood a second longer before it bucked its head and fled into the forest.

In a short time they came upon the campsite. They remained at the tree line with their flashlights scouting the defiled area as though the grounds within were somehow hallowed and not to be entered. The tent lay collapsed in a heap of material, the Styrofoam cooler busted apart. A thin thread of smoke unspooled into the dark air from the old fire, some cookery stood upended on a log to dry.

Be ready with that thing, Fielding said as he unholstered his revolver. Clinton swung the shotgun off his shoulder and clicked off the safety. Fielding levered back the hammer of his Colt.

Allamakee County Sheriff, Fielding called into the night. We have firearms drawn. Anybody out there best make themselves known right now.

They waited. They were answered only by the frogs.

You wait here, John, Fielding said. Just in case.

Fielding and Clinton picked among the debris, toeing at the bloody rainfly of the tent, tin cans sprawled. Clinton waved his light against the limestone wall near the fire pit and found pock-marks where shot had hit. Some lay scattered over the ground and Clinton knelt and gathered a couple in his hand. Fielding holstered his revolver and stood with his hands on his hips, squinting speculatively over the scene. Clinton came over and dropped the shot into Fielding's palm, then shined his light there.

Looks like twenty gauge, Clinton said.

It is twenty gauge.

That doesn't help none, does it?

Fielding dropped the shot back into Clinton's hand like he was sharing candy. Keep em anyway, Fielding said. Never know. Have a look at this rainfly.

He trained his flashlight on the tent. The powder-blue material was stained in a wide oval of blood.

Yeh know what's puzzling me, Fielding said.

I think I might, Clinton said.

He came back for the body, Fielding said. Didn't he?

Clinton sucked his teeth and spat into the dirt.

We better take John on home, Fielding said.

PART III

OSCAR 1960

You could see it after the river fell. Ruined examples of life, portraits of death. The high mark would hold the snared waste that in the near past ran so quickly. That was proof that it happened. Stripped trees and mud-caked briers were scenes of another kind of struggle.

 When the river falls it arranges new trees, still green, alongside ones a hundred years old, bleached white as bone, like a palimpsest marked again. When the river falls and the water runs shallow over the bedrock it's easy to forget what a river is capable of. When the banks reappear and the mud dries out you'll find children swimming in their holes and young lovers picnicking in the grass. The still green trees will be played upon or used as a bench for a man fishing and it will be like a flood never happened, and the river will move on, keeping its secrets. But we're all discovered. Nothing stays hidden forever.

31

They went out County Road Nine toward the river. The deputy drove as Sheriff Fielding pointed out things to Ness in the back seat.

Everything changes don't it? Fielding said. That used to be Olson's Hay and Feed before it went tits up. That open field there was once a racetrack. Stock cars. People complained. Said it was too noisy. Moved it outside a town limits.

Heard it last night, Ness said.

Stock cars came out a Prohibition, Fielding said. Yeh know that? Fast cars to outrun the good guys. Prohibition ends, they don't know what to do, so they start racin each other.

The bootleggers? Ness asked.

I don't know, Fielding said. The cars, I mean. I don't know

who was drivin them. We'll have to go one night. Hell of a good time.

I hear you was kissin on Heather, Clinton said.

No sir, Ness said.

Heather, yeh say? Fielding said. From the hotel?

That's what I hear, Clinton said.

Well, you heard wrong, Ness said. No kissing. Just a little supper. I don't like eating alone.

Fielding and Clinton looked at one another.

Well, Fielding said, be good fer Heather to find someone. She ain't gettin any younger.

Fielding tapped the window with a knuckle.

My deddy was sheriff of Oscar, he continued. And his deddy before him. I don't know what they'd say about all this nonsense goin on now.

They passed a pasture with rusted barbed wire stapled to fenceposts. Cows with their heads hung like puppets and their jaws chewing mechanically. Turned onto the slough road and rumbled down with the cruiser rattling and Fielding holding his cup of coffee in the air. The cruiser pitched in the ruts like a roller coaster car. You could hear the grass swishing the undercarriage. The sheriff continued to talk as though Ness had paid for a tour.

They went further. Remnants of dark weather. Floods that stained the earth. Dry grass caught like dried snot on the limbs of brush. What grew out of that dark earth looked to be drawn by a mordant hand. It was a very bright day but down that road, overgrown as it was, the light was pinched out and it quickly got very dark. They passed a swamp and even inside the cruiser Ness could hear the frogs wailing.

Where we going exactly? Ness asked.

Thought yeh might want a see where them kids were campin, said Clinton.

At the end of the road a line of bright tape. Ness thought there might be some officers or people down there but there were not.

The tent's gone, said Clinton, as though in warning. Cooler ain't there neither.

OK, Ness said.

Jest tellin yeh, Clinton said. Case yeh expectin sumpin more.

So what are we looking at?

Jest thought yeh might want to see the site, Fielding said.

They parked the cruiser and got out and ducked the tape and began down a skinny path. Heat of midday started the wind to move through the trees, and the leaves shivered as though they were afraid of something. They climbed down a sandy bank thick with catbriers. Came to the campsite and quieted as if a vigil were taking place. The trees broke and the sun was flaring on the sand. The deputy and the sheriff walked in a single-file line out toward the water and even in the open the deputy followed behind him. The sheriff started pointing at things in the rocky loam and telling Ness what they'd first seen the night Hannah Dahl was found naked and Billy Rose went missing.

They made camp right here, Fielding said. He toed the remains of a burned-out campfire.

Ness unbuttoned his jacket and knelt and lifted a handful of dark sand and ground it together in his palms. There was blood in the sand and it stained his fingers red. He stood and wiped his hands together.

Where'd the tent go? Ness asked.

We took it down to the courthouse, Clinton said.

And the cooler?

Took that too.

Didn't leave anything, did you?

Found these, Clinton said, unbuttoning his shirt pocket and dropping the shot into Ness's hand.

Twenty gauge, said Ness.

That's right.

Ness poked them around in his palm like he was counting money. Then he gave them back to Clinton. He walked slowly through the campsite with his hands on his hips and his eyes lowered, combing the sand. Fielding hooked his thumbs in his belt and Clinton stood with his arms crossed.

What're yeh lookin for, Clinton finally said.

Anything, said Ness.

You want us to take yeh up to that Sellers place?

In a minute here.

Ness picked up a stick and poked at things in the ground. Walked along the perimeter. Difficult to see but through a tangle of ferns he saw faint footprints coming from the woods. Footprints going in again. He pushed aside a bushy fern and stood there contemplating the marks.

Fielding came over and said, What yeh got there, Ed?

Ness pointed the stick into the woods. This Sellers, he wouldn't happen to live in that direction would he?

I reckon that's the only direction he could live.

Ness made an interested sound, said, Why don't we go see what Mr Sellers is up to.

32

Coming down the muddy road to Sellers's place, the deputy had to stop the cruiser before a barricade of rubble, chunks of concrete, rotting trees blocking the way. A hand-painted sign: NO TRESPASSING.

Seth, Fielding said. Go in the trunk and get my galoshes for me.

They picked their way around the rubble and started down the road three abreast with their feet sucking in the mud. The grass and weeds grew wild. Not a car's tire to ford that stretch in quite some time. The half-gone carcass of a deer lay in the ditch with its head raked back, shinbones showing and the ribs like a bent fork. Awful smell. Little white worms where there was still some meat. Trash began to collect in the brush the closer they came. Rusted pieces of dismembered machinery. A black mattress with its guts spilling out. A flaky chassis of a truck on its side with the paint blistered and the windows busted out and vines claiming it as their own. They passed black lumps of human shit with green flies casting about as though the piles were playthings.

The first glimpse of the houseboat came in pieces through the meshwork of elms and underbrush. Then in full view they stood on the bank with expressions like you might expect. All manner of trash covered the ground from water to treeline. Thorny scrub snared the lighter refuse like obscene garlands. Ness covered his nose with his handkerchief. Fielding called Rigby's name.

Yeh in there Rigby? he said again.

The sun was straight overhead and they waited shadowless under the dappled light for a response.

We're goin a come aboard Rigby, Fielding called. Clinton unsnapped his holster and was taking out his gun but Fielding held out his hand to stop him.

Maybe he's out fishin, Fielding said, throwing his chin to where the skiff usually was. Let's jest see if he's home first.

Down a footpath worn shiny as leather they scared up a long black snake that lunged like a trick of the eye from beneath a bush and poured like a stream of ink into the water. Clinton kicked a rock after it.

Goddamn them things, he said.

Fielding and Clinton crossed the gangplank first. Ness stood on the bank looking at the houseboat as though it would sink. A bright orange kind of algae Ness had never seen before was thick against the hull and pubic clumps of scum hung from the lines that dipped and rose with the small motions of the boat.

An eyeless eelpout twirled between boat and bank with its jaundiced belly facing the sun. Ness heard the muffled rumbling of Fielding's voice on the other side of the houseboat and stepped cautiously onto the gangplank.

He rounded the corner to find the deputy knocking on the plywood door. Cupped boards of the deck loose over the framing. Ness eyed it all with contempt. On the far shore thin trees grew bent, bowed to the water like penitents at an altar. He paused in front of a window. A wide cobweb strung frame to frame, a furry spider hunkered in the center. Ness tore the web away with a swipe of his hand and was greeted by a cracked wooden face that appeared from the gloom like a ship in fog and gave Ness an abrupt startle. Jesus, he said.

He took his handkerchief and cleaned a circle into the window. Cupped his hands to his face and peered in. In the rheumy light he saw the squalor Sellers lived in. Saw the mannequins in various stages of ruin arranged throughout the room.

This guy work? Ness asked into the window.

Does it look like he works? Fielding said impatiently. He pushed past Clinton and banged the heel of his hand against the door. Come on Rigby, he said. Open the damn door. We ain't got all day.

Well, said Clinton after awhile. Can always come back.

I ain't goin to make this trip again, Fielding said. Only way I'm doin it is if he's comin back in handcuffs. He beat his fist into the door again.

Ness looked intently at the painted face behind the window, the lacy pieces it wore. Another doll was bent at the waist over

the table, its panties pulled down to its thighs. He looked back
at the one with an auburn wig staring at him from just inside the
window and his eyes puzzled over the hole bored into the mouth.
Looked as though the red lipstick was fresh. Looked like there
were food stains on her chin.

What's he doing with these mannequins? Ness asked.

Hell if we know, Clinton said. We arrested him awhile back
for stealin cosmetics. Maybe that's what he's doin with em.

The sheriff turned from the door, his face blooming with frustration. The hell with this, he said. It stinks out here.

The three lawmen made their way from the boat, up the bank
and back up the road. From a distance it appeared they might be
talking to each other. Deputy Clinton was last in line and when
his back vanished from view through the trees and brush and catbrier, Rigby stood from his place in the slough, waist deep in the
bursting cattails and reeds with a stringer of bullheads hooked
to his pants, recognizing the sheriff and deputy, but muttering something odd about the third, saying, Got a new Johnny
a-huntin me. And as warm as the water was, Rigby did not move
from that swampy place until they were long gone and he had
begun to shiver.

The cruiser swung to the curb in front of the Luther Hotel and
Ness reached for the handle. Fielding turned in his seat. Clinton
was eyeing him in the rearview mirror.

Say Ed, Fielding said, yeh do me a favor and let me come with yeh if you decide a go down to Sellers's place again. I don't want yeh goin down there alone.

Ness nodded and opened the door.

And Ed? Fielding said. Ness paused on the sidewalk, adjusting his hat. Why don't yeh come out to the house tonight. Wife's roastin up a chicken. Red taters and pearl onions. Corn on the cob. Ain't goin a take no for a answer.

That'd be fine, Ness said. Thank you.

It's the little yella place right behind the courthouse, Fielding said. Come round bout six. I got a bottle I been meanin to try out.

When Ness entered the hotel Fielding faced the windshield. When the car didn't move the sheriff turned and found Clinton watching him with sad eyes. Fielding grinned good-naturedly.

Hell Seth, he said. You can come too.

Out for an evening stroll on his way to Fielding's house. The streets of Oscar the color of lavender in the evening light. Ness paused in front of the J. C. Penney window. Eyed the mannequins. Crossed his arms and stood there studying them. Heard the scraping of shoes down the sidewalk, coming closer. Turned to see a small man hunching toward him down the block, walking with some kind of limp. Odd glasses, wearing a ball cap low against his eyes. Came closer.

Hey, Ness said, holding out a hand. Do I know you?

Man looked up, said, Naw. Yeh don't know me. And went on.

33

It rained all night and well into the small hours of the morning
before the weather broke and the sun came out. A band of red
quaking in the east, rippling like a stampede. A blood dawn. Ness
had awoken once in the night to something like a voice hissing in
his ear. A stalwart darkness. Rain on the windows streaming like
tears. Loud against the sills. Shadows lay stamped over the car-
peted floor of his hotel room. Ness rose stiff legged, still drunk,
and wobbled to the window. The floor at his feet was soggy and
his bare toes wiggled atop it. About to close the window, something caught his eye. Like it might be a hallucination, he blinked
several times to prove it wasn't. A small figure squatting on his
hams under the shadowed awning of the drugstore. A thin coat
pulled over his head against the rain. It was dark so Ness wasn't
sure but it seemed the man below was watching him. Ness stood

a moment at the window, the rain wetting his arms and stomach. Finally he leaned out the window and called to the man below, said, Hey! I see you there! But the man only stood slowly, stowing his hands in his pockets, and disappeared around the corner of the building. Ness closed the window and returned to bed as though he'd just dreamt the whole thing.

A phone call came just after 6:00 a.m. A belting cacophony of bells rousing him from whatever dream he drifted in. Ness lay half-naked in the bed atop the chenille comforter, his mouth chalky, tongue swollen and barbed as a rasp. Whiskey bottle three fourths empty on the bedside table. Ears wailed. Temples boomed like drums. The phone ringing and then it quit. Then it rang again. His eyes labored open and he swung up from the bed in a slow wheel. The sun seemed ungodly bright for that early of an hour and he squinted defiantly into it, his corneas burning and the harsh sour taste of Wild Turkey still on his tongue. He reached to the phone.

Ness? a voice said.

Yep.

Amos Fielding here. Did I wake yeh?

Yep.

Sorry to hear that. Get dressed, he said. I'm comin a get yeh.

Half an hour later Ness sat in the passenger seat of the cruiser, pinching his temples, half listening to the sheriff. He was dressed in his gray suit and his tie loosely done. The stubble on his chin looked like dry skin. Fielding leaned in and, smelling him, said, Remind me not to light a match around you.

The macadam of the county road ended abruptly and the dirt

beyond was wet from the night before and beginning to smoke in the early heat. A high wind had put leaves down like lacquer. A spray of brightly colored finches came from the ditch and sheared off as one before the car. The cruiser jostled down the road, fanning a wash of brown water and mud in its wake. In the distance Ness could make out several patrol cars glittering in the golden light.

We have an incident this morning? Ness asked.

That's the word for it, Fielding answered.

Deputy Clinton had parked his cruiser just above a concrete spillway jutting like a thumb off the river. A white truck with the town's seal stamped on the doors was parked beside it. Fielding pulled in next to Clinton and the two men stepped from the cruiser.

Hope yeh don't get squirmy, Ed, Fielding said, and led them in the direction of the spillway.

Deputy Clinton was poised on the concrete retaining wall, gazing down at whatever was at the bottom. The spillway drained. A film of sludge. A city worker in navy coveralls was at the wheel of the big gate valve. Clinton turned with his arms crossed and his hat propped back on his head.

Well, Fielding said, yeh get him out a there yet?

No sir, Clinton said. Waitin on you.

Well.

The three of them stepped to the edge and looked inside. Fielding shook his head and clucked his tongue. Ness removed his glasses.

Buried to the neck, a boy's head appeared in the mud. His

hair was awash with silt. The skin on his face was bloated and his eyes hung open in a strange dull stare. Fish had gotten at him and the lips of the boy were in threads down his chin. One ear was nearly missing. An awful stench wafted up from the corpse and Ness pulled a handkerchief from his pocket and held it against his face.

When did you find him? Ness asked.

Clinton looked up. I got a call about five this mornin. Jim down there got word that a valve had been opened up, flooding the fields out by them houses there.

Clinton pointed to a row of clapboard homes across the floodplain.

He came down to check on it, Clinton said. Shut off the valve and found the boy buried.

Why don't yeh come on up here, Jim, Fielding called out.

The city worker climbed the bank and shook hands with the sheriff and then with Ness. Fielding introduced them.

So you found him? Ness asked.

Yes sir. Around quarter a five this very mornin.

And that's the boy that Dahl girl was with?

Yes sir, said Clinton.

Ness nodded and looked into the hold.

Well, he said. Let's get him out of there.

In an hour's time they had the body exhumed. The coroner, a stout, barrel-chested man, came about fifteen minutes later. He crossed to the group of men holding a canvas duffel and found the driest place on the ground to set it. He looked down at the dead boy covered in mud like someone might a dead squirrel. The smell was unbelievable and if it bothered him he did not show it. Without a word he knelt beside the boy and, not donning gloves, moved the boy's head in a number of positions. Then he opened the boy's mouth and peered inside. The coroner wiped away the mud and examined his chest, peppered with holes.

The men stood in a bunched line looking down at the body. Their collection of shadows shading it. They didn't say anything. A bird called. The ratcheting of compression brakes somewhere in the distance. After some time Fielding tapped Clinton's arm, said, Why don't yeh give me one a them cigarettes a yours. They were thankful for the smell of smoke.

A reporter came and took a picture, then the body was loaded onto a canvas stretcher and taken away in a black vinyl bag. Ness, Fielding, and Clinton stood on the dike of the river, looking over the shimmering floodplain, smoking cigarettes and toeing rocks with the tips of their shoes, searching for something to say.

34

That night a strange fog, riding the surface of the water like the smoke of a theater stage. A yellowish color, sulfuric odor. Lingered at the banks and was pulled into the forest like wisps of cotton.

Rigby built a fire in the iron stove of the houseboat and set a can of Van Camp's Pork and Beans to warm for his supper. Went about the narrow room lighting what lamps he had. A cavernous gloom. Silhouettes of each doll climbing the walls like crazed puppet hands as each lamp took slowly. The final one he lit, turned the wick too high and belched a gout of soot to blacken the glass flue. Turned it down again. The smell of kerosene heavy in the room.

He carried a lamp to the sink, decided on a drink. Poured himself a measure of whiskey. Took mug and lamp to the low table where a paper bag of new garments stood, and like some deranged museum curator carefully rolled the paper back and looked in at the cherished articles. Took the bag and went to the mattress and pulled out each piece and laid them neatly in display then stood back and put his hand to his mouth for thinking and dashed his eyes between the garments and the mannequins. Decided who would look best in what.

After supper he dressed Mary Belle in a red corset and pulled the black stockings up the smooth thighs. Attached the stockings to a yellow suspender belt. Then bent her at an angle so her palms were flat on the table and one foot kicked up behind. Rotated her head so she was watching him coyly just as he wanted her to be. He crossed the room and went to the door and turned back to her. Then he went outside and watched her through the warped window pane. Dim light and shadows. Oil lamps like candles of a gothic fantasy. Licked his dry lips, said, Yeh know what that look gits yeh.

Fingers fumbling with his belt, he was just about to go back inside when a collection of flashlights and voices came from the dark fog. He shied at the sound and opened the door and took up the shotgun stood just inside. Heard his name called. He waited. Heard it called again. Finally he went around the deck and stood at the gangplank.

Three men spaced on the bank shining the flashlights on him. Couldn't make them out. Only their beams shifting in the pall like mad eyes.

Rigby Sellers? Ness asked.

Rigby stood shirtless cradling the gun in his arms. Ghostly

white, the blue veins coursing beneath like a map. Ribs like weatherboarding under his paper skin. Didn't give an answer.

Don't mean to bother you, Ness said. Just want to ask you a couple questions.

Git off my property, Rigby said.

Now we ain't lookin for trouble, Rigby, Fielding said. Just come by to chat.

I ain't got nothin a say to no one. Now git.

He adjusted his glasses. Levered back a hammer on the gun.

You take it easy, Fielding said. You go any further I'll arrest you for assault with a deadly weapon.

Mister Sellers, my name is Edward Ness. I'm a federal agent out of Minneapolis. Flashed his badge in the light of the beam. There was a boy killed up this way the other night. We just wanted to know if you'd heard anything? Any gunfire or boats back and forth this way?

He stepped down the bank and when he did Rigby's grip tightened on the gun. Ness raised his hands. It's just a question.

Git off my property, Rigby said again.

Yeh know we can go get a warrant, boy, said the deputy.

Then yeh do that.

Ness came closer. He was only a few inches from the gangplank. He could smell the sweat from Rigby. The whiskey.

Nice night, isn't it? Ness said. Odd fog, I'd have to say. His eyes cut to the window of the houseboat. In the low light he saw the angled mannequins dressed in their lingerie.

Do you get fog like this often?

Rigby didn't answer.

You got some company in there tonight? Ness asked.

Rigby shifted slightly. Ain't none a yer business who I got in there tonight.

You want to let me take a look? Ness said, and took a step onto the gangplank.

The click of the gun's second hammer in that night air was like a thunderclap. Clinton went for his gun but Fielding held out his hand.

Ness looked at the gun. Twenty gauge? he asked. I'll tell you what. We'll leave you be. Come back if we have any more questions. He raised his hands again and backstepped toward the bank. You have a good night, Mister Sellers.

Rigby didn't move from the deck until the sounds of the men were drawn like a breath back into the night. Waited until he was sure. Then he went around the deck and stepped through the door.

He looked at his dolls and smirked. They come to take yeh away, he told them, but I ain't goin a let em do that. Ain't no one is goin a take Deddy's girls.

35

His own frayed and concentrated image stared back out of the picture. In the barber's chair, just after his breakfast, Ness popped the paper and folded it lengthwise. In the gray photograph he stood with the sheriff and the deputy alongside the unearthed boy found buried in the spillway. A sheet drawn over. Could have been a discovered relic. A museum's statue being moved. Any evil or wrongdoing existed only in the copy to follow. The men wore blank stares as the camera went off, securing that moment for the annals of history, the men there above their sordid prize, looking neither surprised nor proud. Squinted eyes and shadows told that it was sunny.

That's a hell of a thing, said Lander, whisking warm foam in a cup. He looked at Ness in the mirror but Ness didn't look up.

Yes it is, Ness said.

Lander turned him in the chair so he faced away from the mirror. Tilted the chair back. He doled out the foam with the brush, leveling it across Ness's face.

What's your opinion about all of this? Ness asked through the foam.

About what exactly?

This murder.

I suppose it's like any other.

And what would that be?

Bewildered.

Lander ran the razor back and forth over the strop. Focused on the blade. Looked like he was on the verge of saying something.

Go on then, Ness finally said. What are you wanting to say?

Well, Lander said, there was talk of a mob goin out to Rigby's place.

Ness made a sound, said, Hmm. Lander worked gently at his upper lip.

You think he's guilty? Ness asked.

I don't know, Lander said. But that man ain't right. Gettin arrested for stealin them lady things. I hear he's got some dolls back up in there. God knows what he does with them. I don't know. You was there. You see anything?

I'm not sure yet, Ness said.

Lander eased Ness's head to the side and drew the razor up his neck toward his ear. Blade sounded like it was scraping sandpaper.

You think he'd kill someone? Ness asked.

I don't know, Mr Ness, Lander said, suddenly frustrated. Sit still. Then he said, You don't have children, do you, Ed.

No, Ness said. No I don't.

Maybe that's the difference. The thought that Billy or Hannah could be yer own. You hear about this stuff happenin. You hear about men like Rigby in the world. There just ain't no place for them. Better gone, if you ask me.

36

Against the wishes of the sheriff, Ness drove out County Road Nine. Some ways out pulled off onto the muddy apron of the narrow road leading to Sellers's place. The headlights of his car lurched above the uneven surface, the tires slobbering in the mud. He came upon the heap of rubble spanning the road and parked the car before it. Shut off the engine. The engine ticked as it cooled. And through the glass he could hear all the insects out there bawling like a symphony tuning up. When he opened his door they quit, like their caterwauling was on a switch, and the dark woods went completely silent. Not a stir, not a sigh. Not even the faintest breath of wind in the trees.

He rested his arm on the open door and looked around. It was a black night and morning still a long way off. Gazed about into the lightless woods. He knew not what might be in there gazing back. The car's dome light spilled out over the clumps of spiderwort, his long shadow laid therein, interrupted finally by the bare trunks of elms. One by one the bugs started in again. Chorus of frogs. The lonely oscillation of a whippoorwill. The court-appointed warrant was folded on the passenger seat and he leaned in and took it up and tucked it into the inside pocket of his jacket. Then he closed his door.

A night full of stars. Ness started down the way toward the houseboat, keeping his path to the ancient wheel rut. A narrow strip of inky sky showing between the tall trees, the moon set right down the middle. Leaves at the treetops appeared like a frayed scrim to a celestial theater. He gripped a flashlight but it was not turned on and he wore his .38 revolver holstered near his heart under his jacket with the thumb break unsnapped. Stopped from time to time and held his breath and listened too carefully with his ear cocked woodward as if making sure he was not being followed. Mice in the damp leaves, sounded like distant rifle fire. His heart beat like a foundering ship beneath his gun.

When he came to the river the boat was void of light. Dark and seemingly empty. Could've been abandoned had he not known better. He stood on the bank, waiting for what, he did not know. At that windless hour the stars shone on the water as though the surface of the slough was a plate of mirrored glass. The death of a star ripped through the darkness and Ness saw it both in the sky and in the water as if two stars had been racing and where one vanished into the mud of the far shore the other continued on above, its tail aflame, to burn on till it too reached its end and blinked away forever.

Ness shifted his gaze to the houseboat. He waited for something to move. Confirmation he shouldn't have come alone. A reason to retreat. Instead he snapped on the flashlight and pointed the beam at the side of the cabin. A smudged window caught his light and flashed it back at him. From his spot on the bank he let the flashlight take a preliminary search. Every window closed and curtained. Odd pieces of trash stacked and piled on the deck, a slim footpath through it all. Tires on the roof. Ness said Rigby's name.

Mister Sellers, Ness said, you home in there?

He waited a reasonable amount of time for a response but there was none. Lowered the flashlight to the brush around him. Again he took in the trash twisted in the thorns. Up and down the bank garbage was snared in the lower limbs like jetsam from some great flood. The papered layers of hornet nests. Swung his flashlight out over the water where the beam disintegrated and the far shore lay perfectly still as though it was painted there. He turned to where he'd come from and looked up the road. There was nothing to see but dark trees fading into a darker night but he looked anyway. Then he reached in under his jacket and touched the smooth walnut grip of his revolver. He allowed his hand to pause there, his forefinger tapping the trigger guard as he thought out his next move, and then he unholstered it and leveled it at the house. The whole thing seemed fashioned to scare the child in him. Once more he called Rigby's name. Met with silence.

First step onto the gangplank. Sunk a little into the mud of the bank. Ness stood with a foot still on the shore as if he didn't trust it. Trusted none of it. Then another step. And another. He crossed the gangplank, rounded the bend on the deck, and stood in front of the window he'd once seen the mannequin in. The wooden face was now his own and his own pale image gave him an unexpected chill. He stepped toward the door and with the butt of the revolver banged the plywood, said, Mister Sellers, this is Edward Ness. I have a warrant from the Allamakee County judge to search your residence.

Waited.

Then he tried the handle but it was locked. Tried the window over the kitchen sink but that was locked too. Stepped back and looked the length of the deck. Who's he trying to keep out, Ness said to himself. He walked to the end of the boat where the deck ended. There was no railing so he braced a hand against the cabin and leaned out, but there were no windows and no doors, only the skiff that bumped gently against the edge of the deck.

Back at the door he considered the locked handle and holstered his gun. What he hauled forth from his pocket instead was a small pocketknife and snapping that open he stuck the blade carefully between the door and the jamb and jimmied it a moment before he felt the tip stick into the curved latch bolt and with a quick little twist the door slipped inward a crack and he was met with a foul musty odor. The dust hanging in the light beam lingered then was pulled through the thin opening.

Mister Sellers? Ness said again, this time more quietly. With his fingertips he pushed in against the cheap plywood door and it swung slowly on its rusty hinges. Pointed the flashlight and the shadowline of the door eased across the far wall. What he first saw was the bed. The soiled blanket humped, what looked like the shape of a body. He took his revolver again from its holster and pointed it into the house. Mister Sellers, Ness said, you sleeping in there?

No answer came so he stepped through the door and stood swinging the flashlight around. Just inside the door Rigby's shotgun was gone but how was Ness to know that. He walked over the plywood floors and in some places it was sticky. At the foot of the bed there were two women's outfits laid out, arranged neatly like a mother would do for her children the morning of church. But no saintly attire here. Stepped closer and with a toe nudged the heap resting in the bed. Ness took a corner of the blanket and pulled. A wooden face on a brown pillow grimaced back at him. Black wig, green eyes. A hole drilled for a mouth. Turned to the table and there two other mannequins appeared out of the gloom, seated with plates of cold beans in front of them. Ness went there and studied the similar holes in their mouths, and maybe it was curiosity or maybe it was something else, but he reached to touch the face of one doll, and as he did a sharp clatter came from behind and he wheeled around with the gun drawn only to find a large rat skittering through the open door. In his haste he fell into one of the mannequins and together they went to the floor. Plate of beans spilling, she coming to rest atop Ness. He squirmed beneath her. Surprised how heavy she was. Threw her into the wall and she came apart at the waist. He stood furiously, covered in bean slop. He kicked the other mannequin seated at the table, breaking her hand off.

He searched the place but found nothing incriminating. He'd found the boxes of women's lingerie and wigs and he found a box with three or four baby dolls beside the bed. He lifted one with melted feet out and turned it by its small plastic head, the eyelids of this one peeling open slowly to reveal there were no eyes. It had something inside that made it coo. Purred like a cat. Ness tossed it on the bed.

Walking quickly back to his car he recalled his face in the window over the kitchen sink and he recalled Rigby's face the first night they'd gone to see him and he tried to reason in his mind why his own reflection had caused such a stir when it came to him that within Rigby's face, just as in his own, was the unmistakable mark of fear.

37

Fielding had first seen it in the paper. A town west of Oscar called Harlan. Small place along the border of Minnesota. Seemed a coincidence or perhaps fate, because as Fielding read down the narrow column, skimming from time to time, the phone rang. Fielding said his name.

On the other end, Betsy said he'd a call from the sheriff of Harlan.

Huh, Fielding said. Okay. Put him through. Oh, and Bets, you there? Bring me in some a that cake yer nibblin on. Thank yeh, darlin.

Fielding waited. He sucked his teeth. A voice came on.

Sheriff Fielding?

Yessir. Who do I got here?

Chip Taylor. Sheriff of Harlan.

Mr Taylor. Afternoon. Or is it still mornin? Hell, I don't know. What can I do yeh for?

You can call me Chip for starters, if it's all the same to yeh.

That's fine, Fielding said. You can keep callin me Sheriff.

Fielding roared a laugh.

Nah, Fielding said, Amos is jest fine.

Fielding tapped the paper.

Seems yeh got a brush fire happenin over there?

Well, Taylor said, that's why I'm callin yeh. Heard them boys a yers found a body buried in the mud?

Not my boys, Fielding said. Some poor city worker lookin into a flooded field.

Well, Taylor said, we got someone in custody. Heard yeh have a feller from Minneapolis visitin yeh. Thinkin you and that detective might want to come out and have a look-see.

Why's that?

Feller here said he did it.

Did what?

Kilt that boy.

No kiddin?

No sir.

What's his name? The one you got locked up?

Tilton, Taylor said. Gary Tilton. From Mississippi or some other bum fuck place like that. Talks with a heavy drawl anyways. Found him tryin to fold the girl's body into a trash compactor behind the Piggly Wiggly.

Yeh say you found him?

Nah, Taylor said, manager. Came back after closing. Said

he forgot somethin. Anyways, there he is. Caught like a deer in headlights.

Jesus, Fielding said.

Can I expect yeh then?

You betcha. I'll get Ness on the horn and we'll head over.

Thank yeh, Sheriff.

Taylor hung up.

Fielding tapped the receiver against his chin. Heard the dial tone. Then he hollered at Betsy.

She came in and leaned on the doorframe.

Tragic, she said, ain't it?

Tragic don't even scratch the surface.

He picked up Ness at a quarter to one. Asked him if he'd had his dinner. Then he sniffed the air around him and said, Or maybe yeh drank it.

Just a little nip for clarity, Ness said, and winked at the sheriff.

Uh-huh, Fielding said.

They drove west out of town. Almost immediately they were in cornfields, the stalks no higher than the knee. Fielding commented on it. Said it was going to be a good season. The sky was pale blue and the humidity was thick as honey. Ness wanted to know why.

Why what? Fielding said.

Why a good season?

Grew up farmin, Fielding said.

Thought you said your daddy was a lawman?

Farmer too. But everyone was back then. It wasn't a big farm, jest enough to feed the family. Bring what was left to the market. Knee high by the Fourth of July.

That's the rule?

Ain't even end a June yet. Looky there.

He pointed to the field.

See that? Damn near to the thigh. That's rare. Course that's feed corn and it grows like a weed, but we'll be eatin sweet corn soon enough.

Fielding took a pack of Marlboros from his shirt pocket. Tapped the pack and shucked one free. Held it out for Ness. Ness declined.

Fielding popped the cigarette into his mouth and pressed in the lighter in the dash.

Sara hates me smokin these, Fielding said. Told me they're bad for me. Read a report somewhere. Bad for the lungs. Course the tobaccah companies deny it.

He shrugged.

The lighter popped out and Fielding lit his cigarette and cracked his window and the inside of the car got very loud. Ness took the small flask from his jacket and took a small drink. Fielding eyed him.

I do believe we outlawed such activities in the state of Iowa, Fielding said.

Good thing I'm not driving then.

Fielding took a big drag on the cigarette then flicked it out. Rolled up the window. The smell of the whiskey and cigarette mixed and Fielding said, Smells like a pool hall in here, and he rolled down his window again.

The conversation lulled. Fielding was a talker and did not relish the silence. Sitting with Ness made him a little anxious for some reason. Fielding found it strange that a man ten or so years his junior could provoke such feelings. There was a dark gravity surrounding him, and Fielding began talking, though he'd nothing to say, just to appease it, like someone might down a dark road just to ward off ghosts.

Ness was in a navy blue suit. His shirt had been starched and his tie was in a perfect double Windsor. The harried turmoil of the night before, always within, had been tidied up. It was like making a bed in the morning. A semblance of order. A brittle grasp of control.

Yeh never asked where we were goin, Fielding said.

Figured you had a plan, Ness said.

Ness was wearing dark glasses and his yellow hair was being tussled by the wind.

But, Ness said, if I had to guess, I'd say we're headed to visit the sheriff of Harlan and check out this maniac Tilton they found about to cut up that poor girl.

Foldin, Fielding corrected.

What?

Foldin, Fielding said. Found him foldin her into the compactor. If that manager hadn't come back, he would've.

How do yeh mean?

You ever seen a trash compactor behind a little grocery store? Tiny little things. Meant for cardboard and tin cans. Putting a body in there is an irrational thought. You put a whole body in there, the bones are going to jam it. So you got an irrational mind attempting an irrational deed and when that compactor jams, and it will, that irrational mind will panic and if they can pull it out of there, the only rational thing left to do is cut it up. The only thing I'm not sure of is whether or not that manager was lucky to find him when he did.

Fielding lit another cigarette.

Yeh've given this some thought, Fielding said.

Over time you see a lot of irrationality, Ness said. Maybe it's for attention, maybe revenge. Maybe they've an ostentatious side that craves some kind of notoriety. But even the best-laid plans will eventually fail. Everything, Sheriff, given enough time, will crumble.

Yeh tellin me, Fielding said, yeh don't think it's Tilton? Is that where all this is goin?

I don't know, Ness said. I need to look at him first.

Look at him?

Yeah. Always tells you a lot. The look in their eyes. The way they handle certain questions. The amount of empathy they are capable of, if any. If they did it out of passion, or if they're just stark raving mad. Are they evasive or do they draw you in? Are they emotional or are they calm? Charismatic or awkward? We already know what he did, whether or not he's our guy? Ness shrugged. Like I said, need to look at him first.

Again, he took out his flask and had a drink. Fielding looked over at him, stared as though trying to fish out an answer.

Yeh always been this morose?

Ness flashed him a strange smile.

Just doing my job, Sheriff.

Captured within those dark lenses, Fielding saw his reflection staring back as if from the depths of a deep well, and it had a chilling effect because the relatively youthful appearance of Ness's face masked a false innocence and instead held certain secrets Fielding would never know or even care to.

Fielding leaned to the radio dial and turned it on.

Yeh like country western?

I like everything, Amos, Ness said. I'm in love with it all.

Fielding turned up the music. The pastoral countryside flattened out. Twang from the speakers, a humus wind through the windows. Fielding lit a third cigarette and pretended to enjoy the music and believe everything was going to be fine.

38

Sheriff Chip Taylor's residence was on the second floor of the brick courthouse in the center of town and in the kitchen there was a jail cell. The kitchen was painted a lavender sort of color and a window near the cell brightened up the place. Fielding, Taylor, and Ness stood looking at Gary Tilton while Mrs Taylor fixed them some iced tea. Sheriff Taylor stood at Ness's side with his arms crossed, staring at the prisoner as though trying to figure out what kind of man he was. Tilton had been given a set of stiff clothes, a few sizes too big, that did not fit him well. Two days' time he was supposed to be moved down to the Des Moines federal prison. Across the bridge of his nose and onto his cheek were vicious scabs where the girl's fingernails had gone at him.

Tilton was a scrawny man with buggy little eyes, in his late forties. Grew his fingernails long and had a hard time sitting still. No one spoke until Mrs Taylor had fixed up the tea and left Ness and Fielding and her husband to be alone in the kitchen. Tilton flicked his tongue after the woman like a snake and Taylor rapped his club at the bars, said, Boy, I'll bust yer jaw.

Ness allowed a moment to pass before he said, How did you know that girl you killed?

Didn't, Tilton said quickly. His voice was high and raspy. Didn't know her. Jes saw her and God tell me to do it.

God? Ness said.

Mmm.

Sheriff Taylor spoke to Ness. See what I got here? Give me a crazy man to look after.

Ness nodded, looking at the prisoner.

You killed that boy too? Ness asked.

Yip.

Really? You even know where Oscar is?

The man jerked his head like a marionette. Then looked out the window.

I don't think you do, said Ness. And I don't think you killed anyone beside that poor girl. I think you saw our picture in the paper and for some reason you wanted to be a part of that. I think maybe you want to be someone you aren't. How does that sound? You think I'm right?

The man had begun to rock on his chair and scratch violently at his cheek.

Stop that scratchin, Taylor said, and clacked the club against the bars again.

Is that why you said you did it? Ness asked. You just want some recognition?

When the man didn't answer Ness laughed through his nose and shook his head. Put his hands in his pockets and walked across the small kitchen. Fielding was watching him and did not know what to expect. Ness leaned in to look at a painting on the wall of an old man praying before a simple supper of bread and wine. In the painting the old man's elbows were on the table and his forehead rested in his folded hands.

My mother had this painting, Ness said. Whenever I did something bad I'd look at it and wish I were as good as him. I'd steal a candy bar or get in a fight and I'd come home and look at this painting and think about what I had done. Then I got older. And I realized that's exactly why he's praying. He's praying because he wants to be better. Maybe he knows he can be. Deep down. But this man's a sinner. You see? That's why he eats bread for supper, why he's alone.

Ness turned to the cage and eyed the man.

This painting, Ness said, makes me think about all kinds of sins. Some worse than others. Normally I would say a lie isn't as bad as murder. There are all kinds of lies, aren't there? Like a white lie, that's not so bad. Not really hurting anyone. But this lie, the one you're telling me, this lie is different. You see, if I believe you, if I believe you killed that boy in Oscar, and you're lying to me, well, now we still have some lunatic running around. And I can't let that happen. I can't abide that.

Ness stepped up to the cage and gripped the bars. Pressed his face toward them so he was nearly on the other side.

On the other hand, Ness said, I like this lie you're telling me, because if this murder charge is put on top of the one you've already been accused of then there isn't a way in hell you're going free. Probably will be sentenced to death. Probably will be regardless. Anyway, it's tricky, isn't it? I don't think you killed that boy, but you tell the judge you did. You'll get your face in the paper, you'll have your fifteen minutes. And then they'll hook you up in that chair and fry you like an egg.

Ness let go of the bars and stepped back.

A waste of perfectly good electricity, if you ask me, he said. You want to know how I'd do it?

Ness took out his gun, opened the cylinder, spun it, and then aimed the barrel at Tilton's head and levered back the hammer.

Easy, Ed, Fielding said.

One shot, Ness said. That's how I'd do it.

He pulled the trigger and the hammer clicked. Tilton cried out, a dark oval of urine bleeding out in his lap.

Click, Ness said. He faced Sheriff Taylor. Thank you for your time, Sheriff. And thank your wife for the tea. Sorry to have wasted your time.

39

Sara Fielding was sitting at the vanity in her nightgown with her arms upheld, sliding bobby pins out of her hair. She was talking to her husband through the mirror as he was sitting in bed with his back against the headboard reading the file on Edward Ness the bureau had sent at his request. Read through it, turning pages and then turning back.

Out over the grass and through the wide leaves of the old maple trees rain was falling. The windows were open.

Sara said, How was Harlan?

Still there.

She made a disapproving sound.

What kind of monster tries to put a person in a trash compactor?

Her eyes were closed and she had bobby pins stuck between her lips so she was talking out the side of her mouth.

And in a town like Harlan no less, she continued. That poor manager.

Fielding was quiet. His reading glasses balanced on the tip of his nose. He was in a white undershirt, leafing through the pages.

Amos? Sara said. You listening to me?

What, sweetheart?

I'm talking to yeh.

Fielding lay the folder open on its spine on his lap. Took off his glasses.

What are yeh sayin?

I'm talking about that poor man in Harlan. Having to see that nonsense.

Grim, Fielding said. Mighty grim.

What are you reading over there?

Oh, jest a file.

On?

Fielding took up the folder again as if preparing to read.

Ed Ness, Fielding said. Had the boys up north send it down. There's a dark past here. I want to know more about him. He rattled my cage a little today.

I hear he's kind of charming, Sara said.

Charmin? Fielding said. He had lifted his eyes from the report. Who said charmin?

Oh, just some of the girls. Heather, for example, down at the hotel where he's staying.

I heard that too. Yeh think it was a date?

I heard she had a very pretty dress on.

You think they . . .

Amos, Sara said. You hush.

So jest Heather then?

Heather what?

Thinks he's charmin.

Betsy said so.

Betsy? No.

And Millie.

Millie? The waitress? Fielding asked, confusion in his voice. She's too old for him.

She's the same *age* as me, Amos.

You know what I meant.

And just because he's making a splash doesn't have to mean nothing. He's just having a little fun is all.

He drinks too much.

So he has a vice, Sara said. It's not the worst kind of sin.

There's somethin bout him, Sara. He's got a dark side. He held a gun on that feller we seen today.

On Tilton?

Yes mam.

Loaded?

No, thank God.

Well, next time don't be so forgetful.

She smiled insincerely at him in the mirror.

She pulled the last pin from her hair and then took all the pins from her mouth and set them on the table. Her long dark hair fell like a curtain down her back and she swept it all over one shoulder and began to comb it.

Read me some, she said.

Read you some a what?

The file, she said. What's so dark about it? Let me in.

Yeh sure? Might give yeh bad dreams.

She gave him a look.

Alright, he said. Where to start? Alright, listen here. Nearly beat a man to death durin a breakin and entrin. Was put on administrative leave without pay.

Well, Sara said, the man probably deserved it. Maybe he had a weapon and was threatening him.

OK, how bout this one: ran his car off the road. Drunk as a skunk. Hit and killed three Holsteins.

A what?

A cow. Three a them.

Poor things.

Fielding flipped back to the first page. Ness's height, weight. Eye color. Then, in capital letters: WIFE, LINN ANN NESS (26): DECEASED; SON, PETER JOHN NESS (4): DECEASED.

Says here he lost his wife and son, Fielding said.

What?

Sara stopped combing her hair. Her tone went thin and compassionate.

When?

Seven years back.

How old was the boy?

Four.

Heavens, Sara said. Well, there you go. He's not dark. He's just grieving.

For seven years?

Amos William Fielding. What a terrible thing to say. I can't even imagine. You go wash your mouth. That poor man is in pain and you're questioning him. Shame on you.

I'm not questionin him, Fielding said. Jest wonderin what's got him so . . . so . . . what's the opposite a sunny?

Cloudy.

Yeah, Fielding said. Cloudy. The boy's cloudy.

Well, now you know. Has he said anything to you?

Bout the wife and boy?

Yes.

No mam.

And you ain't going to either, Sara said. That's prying and you ain't no crowbar.

A flash of lightning came and the sky went the color of lime juice for a second. The thunder trailed.

One day it'll catch it, Fielding said.

Sara said, What are you talking about now?

Somethin my deddy used to say. About thunder. Said it was like a dog chasin a car.

No, Sara said, the metaphor is: once the dog catches the car, it doesn't know what to do with it.

I feel like that some times, Fielding said.

Sara stood from the vanity. She was a voluptuous woman. Her nightgown was slightly diaphanous and through it he could see the outline of her figure.

You always catch that car, she said. And you always know exactly what to do with it.

I don't understand the world these days, Sara. I really don't.

Yes, Sara said, but everyone feels that way because every day is new and no one has lived it yet.

Fielding set down the report and looked at his wife. She said things like this from time to time and he always wondered if she had just stumbled upon it or if it was the kind of epiphany she stowed away, saving it for the right moment.

Where'd yeh hear that? Fielding asked.

Nowhere, she said.

That's a Sara Fielding original?

Can't I still surprise my husband?

Yeh scare me is what yeh do, Fielding said.

He tapped the bed beside him. She began to untie her nightgown.

I wish we could've had kids, Fielding said. They'd a got yer smarts, my good looks. Shame.

That stopped her in the middle of the room. Her face fell. She looked like she'd just been told bad news. Fielding knew it too.

Yeh know what I meant, he said.

I know, she said.

She began tying up her nightgown.

What I meant was, I wish we could a had some. You'd a made a good mother. You'd a—

I know, Amos, she said, interrupting him. I know.

She went to the window and looked out on the dark trees. The wind had turned and rain was beginning to blow inside. She just stood there, not moving. Her nightgown beginning to speckle with rainwater.

Come on, Sara, Fielding said. Come to bed.

When she did not move, Fielding stood and went to her. He closed the window. It got very quiet. His bare feet were wet on the wood. He lifted her, cradled in his arms and carried her to bed. He could see she had tears in her eyes and for a second time that night she had scared him. He pulled the covers up and kissed her forehead. He swept back the hair at her temples.

I love you, he said.

I know you do, she said.

He clicked off the light and went back to his side of the bed, and for a long time she was quiet until she said, You be nice to Mr Ness, Amos. You make him feel welcome. Losing a baby ain't easy.

For an hour he lay there watching the dark ceiling. The lightning brightening up the place and casting shadows occasionally. But what he thought about was not Sara or the miscarriages, it was the look in Tilton's eyes when Ness held the gun on him. How a man as hideous as Tilton could be frightened by Ness puzzled him. He lay there trying to work it out like a math problem. Then he got out of bed and called the hotel. Asked for Ness's room. Half a minute went by before the night clerk said there was no answer.

Leave a message, Fielding said. Tell him supper is at six thirty. Tell him Sara ain't takin no for a answer.

40

The car Sellers saw that night could have been any car parked on the county road. Abandoned, out of gas, but certainly empty and vacant of a driver. He glanced at it with only the slightest suspicion as he went about his nocturnal reveries. The rain of earlier had quit and those clownish glasses, catching the moonlight, flashed back like the eyes of some wild animal. Then he went on, a slight hitch in his gait, going on about God knows what at that hour.

Ness eyed him through the windshield. Slumped a little out of sight against the door. With Sellers retreating down the road, Ness sat up. He said, What are you up to?

The road which Sellers traveled had a slight decline. His shabby brogans slapped the pavement like weighted shoes. He

hobbled down the road in full conversation with some appari-
tional companion. Waving his hands from time to time as if to
emphasize a point. Under the moonlight, muttering as he was,
arms flailing, in his soured overalls, he appeared as a child's puppet cut crudely from soggy construction paper.

Ness had put the car into neutral and trailed Sellers
at a distance. With the engine and headlights off, and the
tires rolling slowly over the pavement, the car went forward
in silence. Ness watched as Sellers stopped in the road and
stamped his feet as if in tantrum to something just said. Ness
eased in the brakes, and he was thankful they did not whine
as they sometimes did. When Rigby's mania subsided, Ness
let the car go again, and the absurd game of cat and mouse
continued.

It was like watching someone come to a revelation. Rigby
stopped again in the road. This time the head, with its strands of
oiled hair, cupped between his shoulder blades, turned like an owl
and gazed back at the car.

I never passed yeh, Sellers said. He took a cautious step toward the car.

Who is it? he yelled. What yeh after?

Another step and the car's headlights snapped on and held
him in full view. He was shirtless beneath the overalls and his
pocked skin was the color of mold.

I'm going to run you down, Ness said quietly, and turned the
key. The engine bucked to life.

Believing he had seen the Devil, a ratcheting scream issued

from Sellers. He tore off into the ditch, fleeing into the forest as the tires squealed.

Where Rigby had disappeared, Ness got out and, flashlight in hand, swung the beam across the pale trunks. The caged woods stood motionless. The forest was silent as if all manner of creature was held in contempt.

Come out! Ness called.

He waited what seemed a reasonable amount of time before he called again.

I can hear you shaking in there, Ness said.

He walked to where the pavement met the dirt of the shoulder but stopped there and went no further as though to do so would mean no return. He clicked off the flashlight. Fireflies burned on and off in the fringe of the woods as if trying to light the dark and as a cloud passed beneath the moon, they were the only light.

He waited.

Surely something would have to make a sound. Came finally as an owl's bellow that, for some reason, made Ness picture a lighthouse wrapped in fog. He took out his pistol for the second time that day and levered back the hammer.

Hear that? Ness said. You got one warning.

He waited. The car expelled some exhaust. The radiator fan clicked on.

Then he pointed the gun into the woods and fired. Flash of the bullet and bullet tearing through leaf and bark were indistinguishable. The sudden violence roared into the darkness with the report rebounding endlessly in the hills until it was carried off and the night once again fell silent.

Bullet tearing through leaf and bark and Rigby clasping his hands over his ears and emitting the faintest squeal. Heard the voice on the road herald the warning.

It was only after Ness passed in front of the headlights that Sellers recognized his assailant. Sellers spat a venomous hiss.

I seen yeh, Rigby whispered.

The car started up and drove off, the car farting blue smoke that hung over the road as if too lazy to rise. Engine noise faded and the sound of frogs and cicadas returned. Sellers let out a giddy shriek. Being shot at excited him somehow, like a fetish. Proximity to death or the fragility of life had aroused him.

He lay back in the grass and gazed at the stars through the wickerwork lattice of the forest canopy. I done change my mind, he said.

He judged town a mile or so off.

Reckon I'll pay the city slicker a visit.

Off he went. Scuttling from shadow to shadow. The lights of town rising up softly in the dark.

41

In the glowing blackness of the dream he was set forth on a dirt road that led twisting like a snake into the higher hills where the sun lost its strength and the air was windless and dank and the trees grew to impossible sizes with vines tangled and swaying as if in a strong wind even though there was no wind. On and on. The road became narrow. In the distance he saw a small tinker, burdened with empty tin pails slung like an oxbow over his shoulders. The daylight dimmed in a matter of minutes and as the man was no more than five feet away twilight fell. In the waxen light Ness noticed the tinker had no eyes. He said there was land for sale up the way. Acres, he said. Untouched, he said. Just stay on the road and nothing will hurt you. Ness went on. It became darker. Now and then he stopped to listen for something to make a sound but there was nothing to hear. On and on. Higher and higher. The trees and the sedge among the trees were building like thunder-clouds. Great tendrils reaching upward. From the woods came a cold wind. The jungle of strange trees cleared in front of him and in the clearing where the tinker said there was land for sale, Ness was confronted by a band of emaciated beings, lined up side by side, as though sentinels to this dolorous place. At first they were a thin crease in the distance, like a wave seen far from shore. But soon he heard their yips, and taking in the gruesome sight he stepped back and a darkness absolute collapsed suddenly and he found himself running in the pitch black. Keep running! he yelled. Run! He knew he was yelling at his wife and son but he also knew they were not there. The quarrelsome army yelped behind him. He did not stop running. Out of the obsidian he spied a faint speck of light, like a lantern. He ran faster. He could hear the snarling voices diminishing behind him. The light grew. Not a lantern, but a streetlamp with a few small houses surrounding it. A father holding his son's tiny hand was crossing the road under the light and Ness shouted to them. He called: You have to run! They are coming! The father smiled and held out his hand in a manner of comfort and said: Oh yes, we know. But they are gone now. Do you see? And when Ness turned the horde was gone and the darkness had paled and in the sky were the somber colors of a sunrise. It's best not to go up there, the father told Ness. Then Ness watched him and the boy enter one of the small houses and close the door.

In a start, Ness came awake. He was sweating. The sheets were damp. He threw them off and lay there under the whirring of the ceiling fan. He believed he was still there, on that road with the darkness enveloping him like a tomb. He lay there gulping air.

The moon of earlier had gone and the sky was washed again in a light rain. He could hear it on the window. Just barely, almost like a mouse nibbling in the wall. Maybe it was a mouse. He sat up but saw the window smeared in water. He walked to the window, thinking that might clean out the taste of the dream. At the window he looked through the glass, down at the street. The pavement was slick and looked like oil. It was perfectly still out there save for the stippling of raindrops.

The dream had changed. In a way it was welcomed. In another it was not. It had frightened him like no other, in a way he couldn't comprehend. It wasn't the creatures necessarily, but the place and being in that place alone. The stillness of it all. The quiet that precedes horror.

He went to the bureau. The bottle was uncapped from earlier and he tilted what small amount was left into a glass smudged with fingerprints. It was a relief, it was surrender. He crossed the room. His holster was hanging from a wall hook. He took his pistol and went into the bathroom. He watched himself in the mirror like he was waiting for an answer. His face was jeweled with sweat and he looked like wax melting. The wan light from the street was just enough to see what he needed. Ness set down the glass and opened the gun and dumped the bullets into the sink where they slid like marbles down the steep porcelain and collected in a small hard pile around the drain. He chose one and slid it into the chamber and then closed the gun and spun the cylinder. A little game, he said. He lifted the gun to his head. He did not close his eyes. He pulled the trigger and the click of the falling hammer was only slightly louder than the raindrops pattering on the glass. He leaned into the counter and exhaled deeply. He looked back at the mirror. He scratched his cheek with the barrel of the gun. Then he opened the cylinder and loaded the bullets back in. He set the pistol down and pissed into the toilet and shook away the drops.

Standing in that drawn light he'd the feeling of being watched. The regard of an unwelcomed specter, like the moving eyes of a Victorian painting in some spook show movie. He looked at the ceiling as if it had something to hide.

Crossed the room again and found himself staring out the window. The image through the wet glass was that of a carnival funhouse, with the buildings dished and warped beyond the pane and the few store window lights bleeding in thin runnels of green and red and blue.

He slid up the window. The rain fell on his arms. He looked down on the street. He was looking for something of which he didn't quite know. It was a paranoid sort of feeling.

You've lost it, Ed, he said to himself.

He closed the window and the room was quiet. He went back to bed and closed his eyes and for a long while he did not fall asleep. But when he did he began to snore. No more dreams that night, just the black slate behind which the eyes roll in drunkenness, searching out what they will, seeing things that may or may not be there.

And down on the street, tucked away in the fold of an alley, appearing finally like some gothic fiend, Rigby gazed up at the window of Ness's room and chomped his teeth together.

We learnin bout each other, he said. Ain't we?

Then he skittered away, running on like a child, and anyone awake at that shiftless hour would have sworn they heard coyotes yipping in the night.

42

Ness pulled up to the Fieldings's house around six the next night. A gravel drive leading there and the rocks popped under the tires. A wide porch in the front and all the windows of the house were open and beyond the house was a steep hill full of maple trees. It looked as if Mrs Fielding had set the porch for their supper but there was no one on the porch. From inside the car Ness could see a water pitcher sweating in the late heat and the flies trying to get at a fruit platter covered in cellophane. He sat back in his seat a moment. Then he reached for the glove box and opened the door and took his flask from it and had a drink.

He'd never seen the sheriff dressed in civilian clothing before but that was what he wore. That wide man stepping through the screen door. A pair of khaki trousers and a white polo shirt. His hair was neatly combed and he looked like he'd just shaven. He

came out onto the porch and held his hand up at Ness. Started
down the porch steps, surprisingly nimble for such a big man.

The air was redolent and sticky and birds called in the trees. It
was supposed to rain that night. Maybe sooner than that. Already
you could hear the drumming of thunder against the hills.

What say yeh, Ed, Fielding said. He stuck out his hand and
Ness shook it. Happy yeh could make it out.

Well, thanks for inviting me.

Fielding stood with his hands in his pockets. He rocked back
on his heels a little. Seth, he ain't goin a make it, he said.

Ness nodded indifferently.

The bats had come out, wheeling around in the falling dark.
Almost couldn't see them. Could hear them chirping through
the air.

I wanted to apologize, Ness said.

Apologize, Fielding said. For what?

For the way I acted. The way I acted in the car. The way I
acted in front of Sheriff Taylor. For pulling my gun on Tilton.

Tilton deserved it, Fielding said.

Ness shrugged. No excuse, Ness said. It's not fair to you. To
put you in that position. Anyway, Ness said, waving his hand dis-
missively, sorry.

Hey, Fielding said. Forget it. Over. Done.

Just wanted you to know that.

He ain't the one, is he? Fielding said as though he already
knew the answer. Must've been all over Ness's face.

No, Ness said. No he isn't.

Yeah. Well, yeh come on up. The missus got a nice meal for

us tonight. We'll talk about somethin othern police work. Sara won't have it.

They ate a meal of fried chicken and boiled potatoes, plenty of butter to go around. There was corn on the cob, a lettuce salad with a sweet red dressing, freshly baked bread still warm and wrapped in a cloth napkin. When Ness resigned himself to the fact that he could not eat any more, Mrs Fielding brought out a peach pie with ice cream melting over it and the only thing nicer than the smell might have been the nice look on Sara's face. Seeing how well Ness ate the first piece, Sara dolled up another, almost instinctively, saying she couldn't stand a man with no appetite. Ness complimented her on the crust and Sara said she'd get him the recipe. When it was all over Sara cleared everything away and when Ness offered to do the dishes Mrs Fielding said, Hush, and if she had any pity for him she did not show it.

Supper over and the dishes cleared, Fielding brought out a bottle. Sara left them to talk and they sat alone on the porch watching the night gather over the yard. Fireflies blinking like beacons. Bolls of cotton drifting like satellites. The first mention of rain hissed out over the trees then moved like a tide over the grass. The rain came harder and soon the eaves of the porch began to run with water.

One brandy in and Ness eased back into the comfortable wicker chair. He welcomed the heat of the brandy in his chest and it felt good to not move. He almost felt like closing his eyes.

That wife of yours sure can cook, Ness said.

How yeh think I got this, Fielding said, patting his stomach. And this wasn't a special occasion neither. Pork chops and steaks.

Cakes and pies. Naw, I'm spoilt, Ed. That woman's ruined me to anythin else. How bout you?

He cringed as he said it and he wondered if it was obvious.

Widower, Ness said. You know that.

Shoot, Ed, Fielding said. I didn't mean—

No, I know you didn't. I was wondering when it was going to come up. The boys informed me that you'd requested my file.

It ain't that I don't trust yeh, Fielding said.

I know, Ness said. I'd want to know who I was working with too.

They were quiet then. They sat there looking at nothing in particular. The rain beating down. The wet grass glistening under porchlight. Fielding knew Ness was in no mood to talk about it. Maybe never would be.

That boy out in Harlan was a bit of a nut, eh?

That's putting it mildly, Ness said. It's these copycat crimes I can't understand.

World's changin, Fielding said. Done got itself into a big damn hurry real damn quick. Everyone wants to be famous for somethin now.

My favorite was the God part, Ness said. God telling him to do it.

I tell yeh, Fielding said. I'm bout liable to believe anythin these days. I swear. Nothin seems to puzzle me anymore. Jest when I think, yep, that's bout the craziest thing, somethin else comes along. I've stopped believin that I know the answer.

With that they watched the rain without letting go of a single word. A whomp of lightning set the darkness alight like the

flash of an enormous camera. A scene of trees arrested for a moment. The sky going blue. The thud of thunder came so quickly
it shuddered the panes in the house. Seemed to abrade the very
sky, but whatever it was Sheriff Fielding dwelled on must have
been important because the crack of lightning did not even merit
a grunt. They heard Sara singing in the kitchen, heard her feet on
the hallway floor coming nearer and finally her voice, saying, I'm
headin up, Amos. You boys enjoy yourselves. Then to Ness, said,
And you, you keep him to two.

Yes mam, said Ness. He stood. Thank you for the supper.

You're welcome any time. She came through the door and
kissed her husband on the top of his head. Goodnight you all.

When she was gone and he'd heard the door of their bedroom
close behind her, Fielding said, it might be a three or four kind a
night. Then he smiled warmly.

This bit of privacy and something maybe like freedom
should have offered an opportunity to indulge in the kind of
talk men sometimes do in the absence of women but they sat
quiet as children in church. They watched the rain, hypnotic as
fire. Fielding reached into his shirt pocket where a cool tin of
tobacco nestled against his chest. He uncapped it and hooked in
a finger and laid the wad under his lip. Ness passed on it when
offered. Fielding stood and made his way down the porch steps,
reached under and lifted an old coffee can, his shirt flecking
with rain, tipped out whatever was in the can, tapped it once or
twice against the railing, climbed the steps again, and set the
can at his feet.

Sara don't care for this neither, he said. He spat a gob of the caramelly stuff into the can. Then without the slightest prompt Fielding said, How old are yeh, Ed?

Thirty-five.

How far into thirty-five?

I was born in March.

How long yeh been a detective?

Five years. A week after my birthday. I worked as a deputy before that.

All up in Minneapolis?

Ness nodded. Always wanted to be a part of the law. Ever since I was a kid.

I bet yeh see some interestin things up there in the big city.

Sometimes, sure. Sometimes you do.

My cousin Eli was the sheriff down in Willow, Iowa, Fielding said. That's just south a here maybe ninety miles or so. One of his first cases after bein elected sheriff just bout made him give back his badge. You're talkin a town smallern Oscar. One day in June or July, and this is back thirty some years, maybe before you were even born, my cousin found a foot that had been hacked off with one a them short wood saws and wrapped in the funny papers. He started to look into it but he didn't find nothin. It nagged at him for about a year till he finally got a call from the sheriff down in Des Moines. That sheriff had been callin round tryin to find all these men who'd dodged their parole. He'd called their families, past employers, nothin. He told Eli all the men had been released on bail but for the life of him couldn't find a single record of who'd paid it. Long and the short of it, my cousin toiled over that case for two years, not so much as a fart of anythin worthwhile, till one particularly dry year.

Fielding held up his finger to punctuate that statement.

A warm winter, he said, with almost no snow and only but a few inches of rain in May. Farmers cursed that year but for Eli I think he felt it a godsend. With no rain, the river dropped. A record low. There were parts of the river so narrow a child could step across it without havin to stretch. I still remember the day he called, told me to get down there, that the first body had showed up. Over the next few days it was pretty plain someone had thought of somethin new. Each man had been strung through the ribs with a steel cable and their hands were wired out like Jesus on the cross. Each body was reachin for the next down the line. It was a nasty thing and the smell was horrible. On one side of the river we found a spool all camouflaged in tree branches and such, and on the other there was a crank and the guy must a strung one up at a time then cranked the line into the river. You can imagine how each body looked. The oldest one was almost a skeleton from things eating on it and whatever else. I can't say about Eli, but all my life I won't forget that sight.

He lifted the old coffee can beside his chair and spit.

Your cousin find out who did it? Ness asked.

No he did not.

Hmm.

Got us a possum by the tail, Fielding said.

You mean tiger by the tail.

Nah. Somethin my deddy use to say. Yeh grab a possum by

the tail and they jest go limp. Play dead. So now yeh've caught it but because it ain't doin nothin more, yeh let it go and go on with yer day. Then once yer gone the rascal pops up and skitters away to do whatever it is possums do.

Eat ticks, Ness said.

Huh?

They eat a lot of ticks.

Well, whatever they is doin they keep on doin. I'm tellin yeh this because sometimes yeh don't find what yeh set out to. Sometimes there ain't no answers.

There was a pause. Ness must have been thinking about that, said very plainly, Well, somebody killed that boy.

Sure, said Fielding. That's why we keep lookin.

They didn't speak then for a very long while, just leaving themselves to sit and drink and spit, just staring off into the rainy night, with its thunder in the hills and hidden ghosts.

Yeh know Sara and me had our troubles, Fielding said. Babies, I mean.

You wanted children.

Wanted a whole mess a them. Wanted to watch them grow up here and run around and go to baseball games and school plays, graduation. Give toasts at their weddings. The whole bit, Ed.

Fielding reached down and lifted the can and spat the whole of the chew into it and then set the can back on the porch floor and reached for his glass and lifted that to his lips and took a drink of the bourbon and swished it around his mouth and then sat back and put the glass in his lap and said, Miscarriages, Ed. Five a them.

I'm sorry to hear that.

Takes its toll.

I believe it.

After the fifth, Sara'd had enough, Fielding said. Hell, me too. She got a operation and that was that. I sometimes think we waited too long. I was too busy with other people's problems. That happens. Yeh wait fer everythin to be just so.

Fielding took a sip.

Yeh believe in God, Ed?

No, Ness said. You?

I think so. At least it doesn't hurt anythin to, I suppose.

You might be right.

Keeps me honest, at least. Makes me mind my Ps and Qs.

That's why they call him The Father. Ness pointed at Fielding. And you're The Son.

What's the Holy Ghost then?

The rain, the thunder. I don't know. I don't believe in it so I don't have to think about it.

Ness reached for the bottle but Fielding took it first and tilted it first into Ness's glass and then into his own. Ness looked at the glass, holding it up, examining it.

Peter would have been eleven this year, Ness said.

That's a good age, Fielding said.

I should probably give this stuff up, Ness said, looking at the bourbon in his glass. But not tonight.

Then he took a drink and closed his eyes and listened to the rain.

PART IV

OSCAR 1960

A flood is not always a bad thing. Where the river had been and where the river was going—it cleans things that need to be cleaned. Just like a fire, it scours from the surface of the earth the excess and blight. Things build up and need to be cleared away. People lose possessions and that's a tragedy, but still they rebuild by the river and still the river moves along with the people by its side. Some years are dry, some years are wet, but what's certain is the water moves. A wish could be dropped in the shallows of the headwaters and end up coming true in the ocean. Not everything is buoyant enough to make the journey, but everything, eventually, makes its way to the end. Sometimes the end takes longer for some, and for others, it doesn't stop at all.

43

Three weeks passed. Nearly a lifetime. Night came with a tempest. Such a torrent the houseboat listed. Heeled like a yacht. Thunder in the hills and the slough dancing under the hard rain. A long night. No sleep to be had. Rigby stooped at the woodstove, stoked the fire. A shawl donned over his skeleton shoulders, naked save for a pair of women's panties he had rescued from a trash can. He had cut all of his hair, taken to wearing one of the dolls' wigs. A kind of hacked bob he'd done himself by taking handfuls of the fake hair and slashing it with a dull knife. Rouged lips, jade eyeshadow. Stood back from the fire and spun the shawl from his shoulders like a matador. Lifted a dress laid out on the mattress and held it up to his skin. He flattened the skirt. Shifted side to side in a clumsy sashay. Began to dance. The painted wooden faces watched him with adoration.

He put on Mary Belle's favorite dress. He danced to the music that came through the tiny radio, twirling the dolls in turn. The boat reeled and he danced, danced. The rain drumming on the roof and he danced. How he loved them, he would never let them go. The rain lashing, and Rigby dancing, dancing.

WITNESS #8

We were the ones who come up on it. It was real foggy. Just looked like a parked car. All you could see was the light from the dashboard. It was Tyler who got out to look. He told me, Stay in the car and lock your door, he said. I didn't take my eyes off him. He covered his mouth when he saw what it was. When he got closer to the car he threw up. I didn't leave the front seat, and I'm glad for that, but I could still see the foot of that man. The spookiest part was that the car radio was still going. Been listening to the same station as us. To this day I can't listen to Bobby Vee. I'm glad I didn't get out of the car. Some things you can't unsee.

44

Ness was brushing his teeth in front of the mirror when the phone in his room began to ring. Spat into the sink. Wiped the tooth-paste from his lips with a hand towel.

He picked up the phone, said his name and listened.

After a second, said, What kind of town are you running, Sheriff? Then he said, Give me fifteen minutes.

He drove out to the quarry in the gray dawn. Fog heavy over the grass, the wet road rutted from all the cars traveled to the scene. The first parked car grew out of the murk and another one followed. He turned off the radio. A couple of reporters in long coats were talking and smoking a ways back from the mess. Ness rolled down his window and nodded at the older of the two.

Know where I can find the sheriff? Ness asked.

He'll be up there, the reporter said, turning to point. You

might want to park sooner than later. The whole state's out here today.

Ness parked and stepped lightly through the mud, holding his paper coffee cup as though trekking through waist-high water. A big crowd had formed and Ness tried to press his way through but no one would let him pass. There were several police cruisers with their lights going in the haze like lighthouses on a stricken coast. The stout coroner was there and Ness glimpsed Fielding and Clinton, talking between themselves with their arms crossed looking down at something horrible. Ness went around to the far side and called to Fielding. Fielding looked up and went to the crowd and told them to make a path for the detective. Ness shifted the cup and shook Fielding's hand.

What say yeh, Ed? Fielding asked.

I was going to ask you the same question.

They came around the trunk of the black sedan and Ness spotted the legs of a man prostrate in the mud. He looked there and then looked up at Clinton.

Deputy, Ness said, nodding.

Mornin there, Ed, Clinton said, shaking Ness's hand. How bout this? Got us anothern.

Ness looked down at the dead man. Half his face was hidden in a puddle of brown water and the water leached into his open mouth. Pawmarks of a raccoon where the critter might have tested the opening at the man's neck.

Ness stepped between the man's legs and peered into the back seat. Dark smears of dried blood as if someone had been pulled across and out. Ness leaned in. Looked in the front seat. Looked on the floor. A pair of women's panties balled up and shoved under the passenger seat. Ness took out his handkerchief to grab them.

There was a lady? Clinton asked.

Unless he wears women's panties, Ness said.

Where'd she go? Clinton said.

That's a good question, Deputy. Who found them here?

Clinton raised a finger to a young couple sitting in the back of a police cruiser, urged with his chin, said, Them kids there did. Come out to do some kissin I reckon and come across this.

You ask them about it? Ness said.

Sure did, said Clinton.

What did you get out of them?

About what you'd expect.

They say if there was a gal with him?

No.

They say if they passed anyone driving down the highway? Maybe walking?

Nope, Clinton said. Did say the radio was runnin.

Was the engine on?

Nope.

Ness nodded. Well that tells us something. He sipped his coffee. Was the car registered to this guy? he asked, nudging the dead man's foot with the toe of his shoe.

It is, said Clinton. He pulled out a pad of paper. The man's name is Arthur Foss. Dubuque, Iowa. Aged thirty-eight. Five foot nine inches. Weighted a hundern seventy pounds.

Was there any money on him? Ness asked.

A little over a hundern and fifty, Fielding said.

And it was still in his wallet?

Yep.

Ness glanced about. Could see the fog moving above him, tumbling like sea current. He walked out to the lip of the quarry and looked down into that depthless void, the surface of the water down there somewhere. Nudged a rock off and waited for the sound. Then he looked out into the gray field behind the quarry where a few dead trees stood like bones. A narrow road led through it and in the middle of the road the grass had begun to grow there. The sheriff and the deputy were watching him. Ness pointed.

Anyone check out there? he called. Scratched his chin.

Without a word Ness pressed through the crowd of people and walked out the road till he was standing alone. Grass coming to his waist, beads of dew the size of pearls bending each blade. Looked back at the crowd, looked like a shoal in a bay. No one turned toward him save Fielding and Clinton. Camera flashes exploded without a sound through the fog. Ness looked at the ground, something catching his eye. What he saw was a faint track of footprints, small footed and spaced as though in a hurry. Ness followed them into the tall grass. Disappeared like smoke.

Yeh might have a little bloodhound in yeh, a voice said.

Ness turning to find Fielding kneeling over the tracks in the road.

Fielding said, Just heard he wasn't alone.

Foss?

A girl from Violet's. Miz Rose just called in. Said she's missin a girl.

What's Violet's?

Cathouse on the edge of town.

Who's the girl?

Name's Caroline Tyre.

Tyre?

Like a car, Clinton said.

Ness, pocketing his hands and kicking the grass, said, Suppose we need some real dogs.

45

The night before the crime and the reporters and all the cameras. All of it yet to come. And Rigby haunting the countryside. His breath a kind of whiskey fume. Despite the heat of the night, he exhaled plumes. Like a slathered skeleton horse, his skin steamed into the fog. The moon and the stars swung in a heaven's dance. He stopped in the middle of the road, took a blade from his pocket, and swiped it at the moon. Then he uncorked his hip bottle of whiskey and sank a long drink. Faded deeper. Howled up at the sky.

He went to the whorehouse that had thrown him out to watch Caroline again. It had become a bit of a habit of his. One of many nights, hidden away like some lesser animal, he watched her, knew her room. Some nights she didn't leave at all and he'd watch her move about the clapboard room like a tin target at a carnival arcade. Some nights there were men, some nights there were none. Some nights there were multiple men. Sometimes he'd curse her name, others he'd vow to keep her from harm. Often he'd fall asleep and wake in the gray dawn, cold in the damp leaves, hearing her voice collide with the chittering of birds. He'd peer through the limbed skeleton of the bush as Caroline and another girl walked to their car and watch the red taillights fade in the exhaust and haze, and sometimes he'd shoulder his gun and take aim at her head behind the dewed glass until the car swung out of sight.

Tonight in his preferred bush of thorns, he stayed quiet as a shadow on a cloudy day. When her lamp came on he pushed through the bracken and hunch-loped through the moon-damp grass toward the light. His back against the house. Heart like a timpani drum on his rib bones until the courage arrived. He peered through the thin slit between the curtains and watched her. Naked in the room. Door closed. Naught but a pale thing with her auburn hair tied up, standing before the mirror. Her small breasts weightless with her arms upheld. Dancing like a sock hop. Rigby whispered her name. A whippoorwill sang into the night air as though something might be listening.

Rigby watched five minutes more until she pulled on a light blue dress, did her hair properly, and left the room. A voice, then another, coming out to the porch sent him scuttling back into the undergrowth. His fingernails black with dirt. Dust caked in his palms.

Later, a faceless john escorted her from the house. He'd heard the word quarry as they crossed the dirt lot to his car. Then he heard her giggle and this almost made him cry. A giggle reserved for him. So he had thought. The car passed in the drive, headlights swinging across the bushes, held him in a sickly yellow glow for a fleeting moment then went dark again. He came from the bushes like an emaciated dog, picking the twigs and fodder from his shirt. Gripped the wadded bills he'd brought for her in his pocket like a child does when charged with an important task. He heard the car turn out onto the highway. Saw the lights go spilling into the darkness.

46

He went out toward the quarry road, taking a short cut through the forest. The fog grew thicker and there the moon went out completely. He'd nearly gone the length of the road when he caught the first glimpse of the black sedan.

The engine was not running and despite the heat of the night the windows were rolled up, fogged completely. The car shifted about softly on its tires, a whispering issued from the shocks. An asthmatic wheeze. Rigby stopped in the middle of the road. Let a long moment pass. Then he took a few steps closer.

The outline of a hand suddenly lurched against the inside of the glass and then smeared away. He watched some more. The excitement of the act filled him. Again the hand clapped against the glass. The thin fingertips curled, trying to grip the smooth surface.

Rigby began to make out the faint outline of a shirtless man leaning back into the seat and the cool shape of the girl facing him. The silhouette of her breasts, her exposed neck as she threw her head back. He pulled at her auburn hair. Through the window Rigby could hear the girl squeal and then she laughed crazily. The motion of the car grew. One of them must have nudged the window handle for a narrow line opened and the girl's moans carried into the night, set off the yip of a distant dog. Rigby squatted on his hams, his heart hammering against his sternum. A strong desire to be closer overcame him and he did just that.

He worked his way to a vantage not ten feet away where the grass was tall and sat back on his heels and clutched his arms around his knees and rocked gently. He had a thin wooden smile and he breathed through his mouth like his lungs were tired. The girl said, Ooh, said, Yes. She called the man's name. Rigby undid his pants. And then for a reason beyond his control, Rigby started toward the car.

The couple was sideways in the back seat. The girl was on her knees with her hands on the glass. The man had moved behind her. Rigby's image grew over the window like a cloud blocking out the sun. For a second his face and her face were paired, laid upon each other like layers of printed silk. She wore his glasses, her lips were his own. Then she lifted her face, at first not comprehending, then quickly, like fire catching, saw the hazed hairless figure behind the glass and screamed.

The man, pulling out of her, shouted, Who the hell is that!

Rigby, instead of running, opened the door and the girl on her knees attempted to cover herself. The dome light caught them strangely. The hot reek of the act spilled from the car. She glanced once at his waist, his pants undone, but it was his face, she seemed to remember him. The snaggled teeth, the cartoon glasses. Her mouth opened as if trying to recall a name. All she could come up with, said, You.

The man pulling on his pants, reaching for the opposite door handle, said, You're a fucking dead man!

Rigby moved closer.

I got yer money, he said. He pulled out the wad of bills to prove it. I told yeh I'd owe it to yeh.

The girl screamed again and recoiled, sliding back into the seat, trying to pull up her skirt.

It sent Rigby into a hiss. He lunged like a cat. She screamed beneath him. The warmth of a body new to him. He tried to kiss her but her head kept snapping away. He tried to hold her. Tried to lift her skirt.

But I got yer money, he said. He almost sounded frightened.

He got her legs apart and was about to drive into her when a hand clasped down on his shoulder and wrenched him from the car. A voice spitting venom, You're a fucking dead man!

In one motion, as he was reeling around, stumbling to get his balance, Rigby snapped open the blade and swiped once, catching the man's throat. At first, innocent as a paper cut, a thin line appeared. The man stepped back, eyes wide as dinner plates. He touched his neck softly like he was feeling his glands. Then the two edges of skin became dark and the blood began to purl like oil. The man tried to say something. Only a choked, bubbling sound. Could only stare at Rigby as though waiting for an answer.

Rigby too, staring in disbelief at what he'd just done. The man staggered once, going to a knee, trying to stand, and falling again. With the blood all but out, he tipped forward a final time. The girl screamed. Scared Rigby out of it, and he turned and without a thought sank the blade into the girl's stomach. The girl gasped, went quiet. Rigby sank the blade once more and then a third time. On the third he missed the stomach and landed between the ribs where the blade caught and jammed and then snapped off inside of her. Her lips went red. A stream of blood ran like candle wax down her pale cheek and into her auburn hair. Rigby stood back, watched. Stood there until she went still. Like sleeping with her eyes open, he thought. He reached out to tickle her foot to see if she was faking it. He fastened his pants and leaned into the car and pulled her out. Hauled her like a bag of grain onto his shoulder. Carried her like that all the way home.

That night he laid her on his mattress. Got her undressed. He stared at the body for a long time. Her nipples had gone gray, her freckles looked silver. He brushed his fingers lightly over the wispy hair between her legs. Went to his box of cosmetics and uncapped the red lipstick. Painted her lips garishly, circled them over and over. He laid her on her side and went out the door and looked at her there on his bed, the lamp flame behind the soot-choked glass bringing a little life to her. Watched her for a long while, shivering with excitement. Then he went back in and turned off the oil lamp, lay down beside her, and fell asleep.

Later, he awoke to the sound of rain. The sight of her almost startling. Her naked back was blue in the darkness. Not quite cold beside him, but cool. The tips of her fingers stiff as twigs. Red nail polish gleaming like candy. Her buttocks were pressed into him. He grabbed her hips and pressed back.

I had yer money, he muttered.

It was not making love, exactly, but when it was over Rigby had fallen to tears.

That night he dragged her by the arms into the woods. Her bones loose under the skin. Her head lolled like a dog's tongue. Through the thorns and catbrier, sounded like a bear pulling a carcass. A drizzle was falling. Deep in the woods he set her down. Covered in dirt, her breasts looked like spoiled flowers. He arranged her with her arms at her sides, squared up her feet, said, I'll be right back.

He returned with a shovel and dug a deep grave. He knelt at her side, leaned in to kiss her, and then rolled the body into the hole where she landed facedown. He began to fill the grave back in. Took more than three hours, thought about digging her out again but reconciled the urge. Sat against a tree finally in his exhaustion and fell asleep thinking about her. When he awoke again the sky was the color of woodsmoke and he was shivering.

47

Tyre? Ness asked.

Like a car, Clinton said.

Ness put his hands in his pockets and kicked the grass, said, Suppose we need some real dogs.

Later that morning the baying hounds careened through the woods outside of Oscar like specter calls in a dream. A steady rain was falling. By ten the dogs had picked up the scent and their handlers had to haul back on the leather leashes to restrain them. A mob of men had joined in. A line like hunters after quail. Some of them carried rifles on their shoulders or at their hips and Ness watched their tempers as much as he did the dogs. There was fevered talk. This was not lost on the sheriff.

I don't need a jury to tell me it was him, said one man.

Yer right there, Chester, said another.

A third man said, I heard Jimmy had to throw him out one night. That he was gettin rough with that girl. That's how he knew her. It was from that night. Was stalkin her like a animal.

Another said, He's gotten away with too much by God. We've let this go on too long.

Sheriff Fielding looked over at the group of men, their fingers hooked through the trigger guards, and said, Yeh all settle down.

They looked at him like scolded teenagers.

In fact, Fielding said, give me them bullets.

Yeh cain't take our bullets, Sheriff.

The hell I can't. Give em over.

Fielding put the bullets and shells in his breast pocket. What he couldn't fit he gave to Clinton.

Yeh all can have these back when we're done.

By noon the rain had picked up and slowly the dogs lost the scent. They started tracking off in every which way until all the men began to eye one another. Fielding stopped and called them together and stood there with his arms crossed and the rainwater peeling off the brim of his hat.

What do yeh want to do, Sheriff? Clinton said.

Well. He looked up at the trees and had to squint into the rain.

I say we go to Rigby's, said a man. See what the sumbitch got a say about it.

There was jeering from the other men. A hot thrum of aggression.

Now hold it, said Fielding. I ain't about to let a posse run off and string him up.

If yeh ain't goin to do it we will.

The hell you will, Fielding said. Bill, you take yourself home. Take these others too. Last thing I need is more men to arrest.

Yeh cain't jest let him git away with this, Sheriff.

No one's lettin anyone get away with anythin. I just ain't goin to allow yeh all to go out there like a pack of shiftless animals. Now get on home. We thank yeh for comin out and helpin like yeh done.

The men stirred about, looking from one to the next. Kicking at the mud.

Go on! Fielding said, shouting at them and clapping like one would a pack of dogs.

Reluctantly, they broke away in pairs. They looked like ghosts in that damp wood, wandering on, evaporating in the mist. Ness, Fielding, and Clinton stood in a loose circle facing each other. Fielding closed his eyes and pinched the bridge of his nose. The rain was loud on the leaves.

You know they're just going to go see him for themselves, Ness said.

Fielding spat to the side. Yeah, I know.

What do yeh want to do, Sheriff? Clinton asked.

Fielding looked around, said, I want a get out a this rain.

That same afternoon, July the twenty-fourth, 1960, Sheriff Amos Fielding issued a statement to the town of Oscar, Iowa, calling for the arrest of Rigby Sellers in conjunction with the suspected murders of Caroline Tyre, Arthur Foss, and the boy, Billy Rose.

Within the hour the sheriff's office had calls coming in from townspeople claiming they saw Rigby trying to hitch out of town. Saw Rigby tramping down the railroad tracks. Saw Rigby heading for the state line. Some calls differed so greatly that they put him some forty miles apart at the same time. The state police got involved and troopers from as far south as Fort Madison patrolled the highways and the back roads. Even had a patrol cruiser stationed out front of the berm of rubble leading to Rigby's place in case he was foolish enough to return.

Many times in the following days Ness and Fielding and Clinton walked the short distance to the houseboat but nothing had changed. The townspeople grew impatient. No surprise. And soon there was some rather aggressive talk on how to handle all of this.

48

They saw them coming down the road like something out of an old-time movie. A heavyset man named Bly headed up the posse. Carried a rifle in one hand and a lantern in the other. Each man the same. The flames and the shadows from the flames danced on each face. Their eyes were hidden under their hats. Wicked talk spread among them like grassfire. Turning down the rutted road their flashlights caught the metal paneling of the cruiser. The lawmen in their rain slickers standing with austere looks, expecting this the whole time. Fielding and Ness shined their flashlights at the men.

What'd I tell yeh boys about this, Fielding said.

They were quiet for a moment, shifting on their feet in the mud. The rain hissed against the hot glass of the lanterns.

Go on home, Fielding said. This ain't worth yeh all goin to jail over. Let us do our jobs. Yeh all get on home.

Sheriff, Bly finally said. We ain't goin to allow this in our town.

That ain't up to you, Bly, Fielding said. Yeh all are about to put me in a uncomfortable spot.

He raped that gal in that car! someone called out.

Yeh don't know that, Fielding said. We don't even know if she was in the car.

Well he kilt em! Slit that man's throat!

Yeh don't know that either.

Kilt Billy too!

Bly said, Ain't yeh goin to let us at least jes go on down there and see if he's home?

No I ain't, Fielding said.

He's trying to protect you, Ness said.

Fielding looked at Ness with a great amount of gratitude and then looked away again before any of the men could tell that it was so.

A fat man named Chester stepped forward from the mob and began to spit accusations. You stay out a this yeh sumbitch. Ever since yeh come round yeh been in the sheriff's back pocket workin him like a puppet. If yeh spent a little more time policin and a lot less drinkin, we wouldn't even be here.

You settle down, Chester! Fielding said. Don't go sayin somethin yeh can't take back.

I ain't sayin it to you, Chester said, I'm sayin it to him. He's a drunk! It's cloudin his judgment! He's either drinkin or diddle fuckin that Heather gal from the hotel.

Goddamnit, Chester, Fielding said, keep yer mouth shut.

Chester pointed his finger at Ness. Yeh git yer ass out a this town, he said. And you stay gone.

A murmur of agreement rippled through the men.

Chester, Fielding said impatiently. I swear it, you make another remark like that and I'll arrest yeh for threatenin a officer. Goes for all yeh. Now if you don't disperse I'll have Clinton here place yeh all under arrest for unlawful assembly. Go on home. All of yeh!

They stood there in the muddy road, regarding one another, the rain burning on the steaming lanterns.

So what're yeh goin to do about all this? Bly asked.

Goin to stay here till he comes back, Fielding said. Then we'll go down and have a talk.

So he ain't home, someone said.

I never said that.

Then where is he?

Just go on home. I don't want to have to tell it again.

When none of them moved, Fielding said, All right. Deputy, place these men under arrest.

Clinton started toward them and Bly raised his hands.

Fine, he said. Jest know we was tryin to help is all, Sheriff. That's all we was tryin to do.

Noted, Fielding said. Now go home.

Like some reduced peasant revolt they sloshed about gazing dumbly through the rain and finally turned and marched out the way they had come, their lampfires and flashlights winking out one at a time as the road bent into the forest until there was nothing but darkness and rain.

Thanks for that back there, Fielding said to Ness.

I guess the place is starting to grow on me, Ness said.

49

The fire engulfed the houseboat sometime around one in the morning and by one thirty the roof collapsed. Smoke so black it could be seen in the darkest hour of night. A toxic smell of burning tires, plastic, God knows what else. When the sun rose it was drumming rain on a mound of smoking black embers.

By eight thirty in the morning a crowd had gathered. Some children stood on the banks watching their fathers step carefully among the tilting ash, poking into the mess with shovels and sticks. Charred debris swirled out in the water of the slough. Reeked of gasoline and shit. Townsmen and troopers walked with handkerchiefs and bandanas tied at their faces and probed for signs of Rigby's body.

Fielding and Ness arrived around nine and stood in a line on the bank looking over the search like sexton foremen. They saw

Bly and Bill and Chester walking about and when they passed Fielding with their hands and boots covered in soot they nodded and said, Sheriff, without the slightest amount of guilt or remorse.

Clinton came up the bank in tall rubber boots and shook hands with Fielding and with Ness.

Well? Fielding said.

Nothin yet, said Clinton.

Do we know how it started?

With a match, I imagine.

Any sign of arson? Ness asked.

Clinton turned. Held a hand up to the wreckage. A look of chagrin, said, How the hell would I know?

Something tells me he's not in there, Ness said.

Fielding nodded. I'm gettin that feelin too.

They watched longer. Smoldering embers being tilled like dirt. Fielding gestured at the men poking around with sticks. Why don't yeh all get some spades, he called to them. Brought some down in the trunk.

A few men began stepping off when someone called, Got sumpin here!

At first sight it looked like a bloodless human leg but they quickly learned it was not. The mannequin was burned badly but still wearing the carnelian smile painted on from before. They exhumed it and laid it out and stood with their spades in their hands, guessing at the holes. The children stopped playing at the sight of the doll and looked on with a kind of mesmerized fascination. Men piled onto the listing platform and peered down at the lifeless form and no one knew what to say at all.

Keep digging, Ness called. Should be two of those things in there.

The men turned. Bly said something under his breath to the others. Some of them laughed. None of them continued to dig.

Fielding looked at Ness, said, I guess we'll have to wait.

WITNESS #9

Yer askin if I knew anything about him? No sir, mister. My little brother and me hunted out there sometimes but we never seen no one. I dared him to go knock on the door once but he wouldn't do it. A boy from school said he went inside. Said that he kept dead people in there. I told him he was a liar. Told me if he was such a liar then I should go out there and prove him wrong. And I was goin to too but it burned down before I could. Pa doesn't like us to hunt out there anymore, so we don't.

50

One more night. A day or two after the fire. No word on Rigby. Like he just up and vanished. Together Fielding and Ness drove around the hillsides and said little to one another outside of the fire and the murders and the unlikelihood of it all and then Fielding made a comment, something like, Suppose ye'll be headed back soon then?

We'll have to see, Ness said. He didn't just disappear. And anyway, like I said, the place is growing on me.

Still got to take yeh to one a them stock car races, Fielding said. Almost August, after all.

I heard them again the other night, Ness said. Loud things, aren't they?

You bet.

Then Ness said, Yeah.

Then he said, I ever tell you about how I taught Peter how to throw a fastball?

Yer boy could throw a fastball at four?

Sure could.

The hills rolled on green and fertile and they drove on and that afternoon, with the long shadows over the river and the clouds leaping into the sky, the desire for a drink left him like rain suddenly quitting and the sky breaking apart into sunshine. There was nothing to explain it.

The next morning Ness went down to Deb's Café and ordered a cup of coffee. Millie came over and Ness said to her, Doesn't it ever stop raining here?

One a them wet years, she said.

He sat there with the hot mug between his hands and watched out the window. When he was done with that he ran across the street back to the hotel and found Heather at the desk and when she saw him she smiled because she seemed to know what was on his mind.

I'd love to, she said. Yeh want to eat here again?

Your choice, Ness said. Figured you might enjoy a night away.

Okay, she said. But it'll have to be tomorrow. I got to work tonight.

Tomorrow's fine, Ness said. There's still that kiss, you know?

Back pocket, she said.

Maybe you cash that in?

Maybe I do.

I'll take a maybe.

He was leaning against the counter but now he stood up straight and fixed his tie.

Six thirty again? she asked.

Let's make it five, Ness said. We've got some catching up to do. Like the sound of that?

Sounds like music, Mr Ness, she said.

Ness in a blue suit, a tan overcoat that reached his shins, tall rubber boots for the mud. He drove down the long road that night in a dark rain through dark woods toward the burned-out houseboat. Troubled by the events. How it all turned out. Something, he thought, just isn't right. Told it to Fielding and Clinton earlier that day, said, I'm going to go poke around a bit. I'm not sold. He didn't just disappear. He'll be back. There's something he forgot. I just know it.

That boy's gone, Fielding said. Gone as a ghost.

The car ticked as it cooled. Rain fell on the brown hood of the Plymouth. Ness strained against the wheel. The scene a sallow yellow in the headlights. The windshield stippled with rain. He drummed the dash.

You didn't just disappear, he said aloud.

He opened the door. Not a bird, not a voice. A stillness like that of the womb. Only the whisper of rain. The hush of the river. He made his way through the mud. A flashlight that seemed to hide more than it revealed.

Ness came to the bank of the river, panning the light about. The remains of the houseboat were heaped like coal. The thing was half-sunk. It pulled awkwardly on its lines like it was straining to leave. Days of rain had flooded the slough. What remained looked like a trash barge waiting to be towed away.

Tucked in the bushes was Sellers's old gangplank. It was slick with grime and waterlogged. Moss like green fur. Ness lifted it with some effort, once or twice slipping from his grip. Got it laid in place finally over the swirling water. Hands filthy with slime the color of molasses. Like a comedic carnival act, Ness leaped gracelessly onto the deck, the toe of his left boot splashing the water. His shin taking the force. He fell to his side, clutching his leg. He winced at the pain. Son of a bitch, he said.

He limped over the heap and started poking around with an oak branch. Lifting this and that. Stabbing at artifacts like a clumsy archeologist. A roaring sound and he looked up to find the swollen river uprooting several old trees. The high limbs swayed like a giant hand was shaking them. One of the great trunks snapped with a boom. Then they were toppled and carried away downriver. The rain crashed down.

Ness stood on the heap in the center of the boat. The rainwater peeled from the round bill of his hat, running like a spigot every time he lowered his head. He stepped cautiously. Lancing the black, sodden timbers. Where Sellers's bed once was he stuck his stick into what felt like wet kelp. Pulled the stick free. Strands of fake hair clung to the point and Ness pulled a black wig from the ashes. Found another, this one blonde. Found a whole box of them wrapped in soggy cardboard. The collection looked like a dead animal. Then he struck something else. He jabbed it again. The sound was like tapping a bowling ball. Ness knelt with a little bit of pain, favoring his bad leg, and pushed his hat back on his head and wiped his nose and put the flashlight in his mouth and began to dig with the point of the stick until the stick wedged into something and broke off. Ness began digging with his hands. It didn't take long. Like a thick quill, the sheared point of the stick was embedded in the hole of a mannequin's mouth. He took the flashlight from between his lips. He wiped at the wooden face. He was careful about it. The cheeks were almost soft. He could see tiny concentric marks where Sellers had taken fine grit sandpaper and polished those cheeks till they were smooth as porcelain. Wiped away the ash, the soot. Streaks of black coursed her face as he did. Took his handkerchief from his pocket, spat into it, and began to wipe her cheeks. Wiped her lips, her nose. He pushed away the debris around her eyes. She was the one he'd seen behind the window that first day. Said, You were his favorite, weren't you?

The painted blue eyes stared up at him, streaming in the rain.

Then it came. A commotion behind him. Almost a snarl. Ness had only enough time to turn with the flashlight. The small impish figure. Coke-bottle spectacles. Hatchet in hand.

Darkness.

51

At some point the next day a phone call came. Fielding on the other end. Sitting in his office in the courthouse. Tapping a finger impatiently. The hotel operator came back on.

I'm sorry, Sheriff, she said. He doesn't seem to be there at the moment. Hope he didn't run off. We got plans tonight.

No kiddin?

No sir.

Ain't that good of yeh. Well thank yeh anyway, Heather. Yeh call me right away if yeh see him, okay?

It didn't stop raining that day and it didn't stop for a week straight. Amos Fielding and Seth Clinton drove out daily to the burnt houseboat to see if Rigby had returned for anything but each day the same. Fielding called the hotel each morning and every afternoon and Heather told him he never showed for supper and that she hadn't seen him since and that housekeeping said his room looks to be untouched.

His stuff still there? he asked.

Yes sir, she said.

Huh. Well, thank yeh anyway, dear.

Fielding and Clinton went out to the houseboat again and went as far as stepping onto the wreckage and poking around. For what, who knows. Some places, they commented, looked to have been dug up and then smoothed back over.

Clinton said, Yeh want a get a couple shovels? A few places here look like somethin might be buried.

Suppose we should, Fielding said.

Back at the cruiser Clinton popped the trunk and lifted two spades. Handed one to Fielding. Walking back toward the river, Clinton asked, Ever get a hold a Ness?

Not a word. Even called up to Ronnie in Minneapolis. They haven't heard anythin neither.

Bit of a shifty guy, Clinton said. If yeh ask me. Off on a drunk maybe?

I'm startin to wonder myself.

Fielding stepped lightly off the bank like he was stepping onto ice. Even under the small weight the platform listed, one corner sinking into the water.

Yeh be careful, Clinton said.

In the middle of the wreckage, Fielding eyed the spot where the embers and soot looked to be smoothed over. Fanned at the edges, dished out with a reckless hand. About six feet long.

Three feet wide. About the shape of a grave. Fielding aimed the point of the spade in the center, about to stab it in, when the cruiser's radio squelched out. Fielding stopped, spade poised in the air.

Sheriff! Clinton called out. Got a car wreck out on Nine.

They can't get anyone else?

Called in by name, yeh were.

Fielding stuck the spade into the mess near his feet. Stood looking down at it. The radio squawked again.

Sheriff? Clinton said. They're callin for yeh.

It kept raining that day. And it kept on raining that night. On the Friday of that week the river rose against its banks and spilled the dike. Most of the town flooded, debris in the streets. The mayor closed all of the smaller bridges on the outskirts of town and a group got together to sandbag the south end. River kept rising. Farms lost crops and livestock, and the farmers would lie awake listening to the rain on the roof, praying it to quit. When it finally did the townspeople came out and squinted at the sun and said, Thank God.

It'd been nearly two weeks since the fire and still no word of Rigby Sellers or Edward Ness. When the river finally dropped Clinton and Fielding went down to the slough one more time, and the bank where the houseboat once was moored was empty. Not even the frayed lines that kept it. In the bright sun Fielding took off his hat and scratched his head and he had to laugh. All the garbage in the water and all of it that had been on the shore was gone.

Just clumps of catbrier and dogwood caked in gray mud. Even the shoreline had changed. Fielding put his hat back on, sucked through his teeth.

Wife's makin a cream pie tonight, he said to Clinton. You better come over for a slice. That woman hates seein pie go uneaten.

They watched the river, witnessing both the past and future in its waters, toiling over the exact moment that defines what it means to live and what is behind and what is still to come. The limestone bluffs rose up on the far shore. And somewhere, deep within the hills, a whippoorwill called.

ACKNOWLEDGMENTS

None of this would have ever been read, let alone seen, if it weren't for Jarret Middleton, who introduced me to my editor, Harry Kirchner. Jarret is one of those rare kinds of artists who is as talented as he is generous; I'm lucky to call him a friend. As for Harry, it is not hyperbole to say he changed my life. He took this book in its early form to Counterpoint and fought hard for it. Throughout the editing process he was selfless and confident and patient when often I was not. He was my cornerman through all these rounds, and he could always stop the bleeding. An elated thank you to Dan Smetanka for all the guidance, and to Rachel Fershleiser, Alisha Gorder, Katie Boland, Wah-Ming Chang, and everyone at Counterpoint for their tireless efforts.

I want to thank Glen Chamberlain for convincing me to write all those years ago, and for her grace and love in all the years since. For all the evenings talking craft and books and relationships and good whiskey, for being a mentor, friend, mystic, and savior. You mean the world to me. Thank you also to Tom Barrett, her husband, who makes the best old-fashioned, who tried his best to teach me to rope.

I want to thank Jonathan Evison, Molly Gloss, Peter Geye, Joshua Mohr, Urban Waite, Sarah Gerard, Shann Ray, Tod Goldberg, and Ivy Pochoda for their early reads and support—your kindness is a fire on a cold day.

Thanks to Jenny Schumacher who asked a question no one had ever asked me. Thanks to Leif Haugen who taught me how to hitchhike and how to pick out a good book. Thank you to my dear grandmother, Norma, for giving me the Smith Corona typewriter I still use every day. Thanks to Andrew Hedrick for being the best bud a guy could ask for, and to Rialin Flores for listening to me read aloud work destined for the bonfire. Thanks to Cosmo Langsfeld, a brother in many ways, for always calling me out on my shit. Thanks to Abram Anderson and Abbie VanDonge for their encouragement and for reading an early draft, and especially to Abbie, who was the first person to quote me back to myself. Thanks to Doug and Suzanne Bizer for reading an early draft and especially to DB for properly pronouncing Detroit and to Suzanne for putting up with DB. God bless her.

Thank you, Mom and Dad, for letting me talk endlessly about writing and books and God-knows-what else, and for doing so happily, unwaveringly. Your love is like a kind of sea one could never reach the bottom of. To my brother, Jon, who wanted to hear a spooky story, which started the boulder rolling.

All my love to my boys, Tøren and Anders. Thanks for letting Daddy go out to the studio each morning. You two melt my heart. To Roddy, thanks, old boy, for letting the kids try to ride you like a horse.

And finally, unequivocally, to Madeline: my water during a drought, my sun after a storm.

DANE BAHR was born in Minnesota. He lives in Washington State with his wife and dog, watching his sons and orchard grow.